Maggie Bean in LOVE

TRICIA RAYBURN

m!x

ALADDIN M!X

NEW YORK   LONDON   TORONTO   SYDNEY

ALADDIN M!X

An imprint of Simon & Schuster Children's Publishing Division

1230 Avenue of the Americas, New York, NY 10020

First Aladdin M!X edition December 2009

Text copyright © 2009 by Tricia Rayburn

All rights reserved, including the right of reproduction in whole or in part in any form.

ALADDIN is a trademark of Simon & Schuster, Inc., and related logo is a registered trademark of Simon & Schuster, Inc.

ALADDIN M!X and related logo are registered trademarks of Simon & Schuster, Inc.

For information about special discounts for bulk purchases, please contact Simon & Schuster Special Sales at 1-866-506-1949 or business@simonandschuster.com.

The Simon & Schuster Speakers Bureau can bring authors to your live event. For more information or to book an event contact the Simon & Schuster Speakers Bureau at 1-866-248-3049 or visit our website at www.simonspeakers.com.

Designed by Karin Paprocki

The text of this book was set in Garamond.

Manufactured in the United States of America

1109 OFF

10 9 8 7 6 5 4 3 2 1

Library of Congress Control Number 2009925472

ISBN 978-1-4169-8700-0

ISBN 978-1-4169-5591-2 (eBook)

For Aunt Marion

1. Maggie Bean stood at the greeting-card end of the stationery aisle, biting her lip and carefully deciding which sentiment would leave the best impression. "Thinking of You" and "Just Saying Hello" were definitely more appropriate than "Happy Birthday" and "Get Well Soon," but that didn't make the selection much easier. On the outside, those cards, the ones decorated with purple flowers and smiling cartoon puppies, seemed perfectly, innocently sweet. But on the inside, with messages like "I treasure our time together" and "Your smile illuminates my soul" written in elaborate script, they were total sugar overload. And since Arnie and Maggie had probably already consumed enough sugar to fuel the Hershey's factory for an entire year, none of those cards would work as *the* card—the one Maggie planned to give Arnie in honor of their very first date.

"Found it."

Maggie took the card Aimee held toward her, looked at it, and handed it right back.

"You didn't even read it," Aimee protested.

"I didn't have to," Maggie said.

"But it could be the one that says exactly what you want it to. It could be the card that keeps Arnie smiling for days. It could be the start of something truly magical."

"It could be," Maggie agreed. "Which is why the glitter is so unfortunate."

Aimee's mouth dropped open like they were eight years old and Maggie had just suggested Santa Claus was a figment of the mall. "You don't like *glitter*?"

"Or feathers, sequins, plastic gems, and 3-D cutouts." Maggie pointed to examples of what to avoid on the rack.

"But, pretty, sparkly cards are the only ones I *give*," Aimee said quickly, apparently still in shock. "Pretty, sparkly cards are the only ones you've gotten from me for every birthday and major holiday in the entire history of our friendship."

"And I love them all!" Maggie clarified. "But . . . I'm a girl."

"Ah." Aimee slid the card back in its slot. "Well, I hate to say it, Mags, but if you're trying to find a boy card, you've got a tough job ahead of you. Boys don't do cards."

Maggie looked away from the rack to face Aimee.

"They do e-mail. IMs. Text messages. Sometimes phone calls—but only when absolutely necessary, and always under five minutes."

"We give my dad cards all the time—"

"He's your dad," Aimee said simply. "Not a thirteen-year-old boy who wouldn't even know how to seal an envelope if his mother didn't lick it for him."

"And you couldn't have brought this to my attention half an hour ago?"

Aimee shrugged and grinned sweetly. "Who am I to stand in the way of true love?"

True love.

Her face burning red at the thought, Maggie swallowed and turned back to the rack. That was one greeting card category she'd eliminated immediately—no need to consider "You're the love of my life," "I never knew love until I knew you," or "I love you, I love you, I *love* you!" when she and Arnie hadn't even been to the movies by themselves yet.

"Be right back," Aimee said. "I told my dad I'd pick up some stuff for him."

"Could you grab some purple highlighters?" Maggie asked, somehow managing to think of something besides her almost-first boyfriend (fingers crossed) for one second.

Aimee eyed the shopping basket at Maggie's feet. "Seriously?"

Maggie looked down at the basket overflowing with notebooks, folders, pencils, pens, erasers, index cards, Wite-Out, paper clips, rubber bands, glue, and Post-its. A pack of pink, yellow, green, blue, and orange highlighters sat precariously on top of the pile.

"I need purple," Maggie explained. "It's the color I use for SAT vocabulary words."

"Even though—"

"The SATs are still four years away?" Maggie finished. "Yes."

"Can I also grab *People* magazine for you? So you can enjoy a healthier work-life balance?"

"If you must." Maggie grinned as Aimee headed down the aisle. They both knew her work-life balance was the best it'd ever been—and about to get even better.

Which was why the card was so important. Next to Aimee, Arnie was her best friend. They'd been through a lot together in the past year. After meeting at Pound Patrollers, where they'd bonded over being the only kids in a circle of middle-aged chocoholics, Arnie had helped Maggie survive embarrassing weight-loss meetings, chocolate relapses, and family turmoil. And two weeks ago, at her family's housewarming party, he'd confessed what she probably should've known but had been too distracted to notice.

Arnie liked her. As more than a friend.

And now they were going out. Or, at least, they were *about* to go out, on a date.

Arnie had given her a beautiful silver bracelet with an aquamarine stone at her family's housewarming party, and in honor of their first date, she wanted to give him something in return. Something that said, "Thank you for being my friend. Thank you for putting up with me when I wasn't the easiest person to put up with, and for liking me despite everything I don't like about myself. Thank you for being supersweet and funny and adorable. Thank you for being you, and for wanting to be with me. I promise to be the best girlfriend *ever*."

"Hey, Maggie."

Maggie looked up to see Anabel Richards and Julia Swanson, cocaptains of Water Wings, their school's synchronized swim team, standing near the "I'm Sorry" greeting card section. They were still tall, thin, and dressed like they'd just left an *InStyle* cover shoot. Their skin glowed a deep, warm gold, most likely because they'd spent their summer vacations lounging on some European beach. This time last year, unexpectedly seeing them here would've been enough to make Maggie freeze. That, or run from the drug-store before they noticed her.

But that was then, and this was now. They were about to start eighth grade. Why not start with a clean slate?

"Hi." Maggie offered a small smile.

"Hey," Julia said again, shooting Anabel a look, like she hadn't expected Maggie to respond.

"How was your summer?"

"Great!" Julia's voice was unnaturally bright.

"And yours?" Anabel asked.

"Also great," Maggie said. "Thanks."

Anabel nodded, and her eyes darted toward Julia. When Julia continued to smile without speaking, Anabel gave her a quick elbow jab.

"Okay." Julia exhaled sharply, like Anabel's jab had reminded her to breathe. "We've been *dying* to know."

"Dying," Anabel agreed. "All summer."

Maggie paused. "Dying to know what?" She knew there was no way *she* had the information they'd apparently been waiting for.

Julia and Anabel exchanged wide-eyed looks, as though each silently begged the other to answer.

"About your *boyfriend*!" Anabel finally exclaimed.

So much for starting fresh. Immediately embarrassed for

being put on the spot—and not even sure what they were talking about—Maggie felt her cheeks burn and her pulse race. A year later and the most popular girls in school still had this effect on her, like she still weighed more than the two of them combined, and longed to live up to their superficial standards.

"Which one?"

Maggie spun around, relieved to see Aimee headed their way. When she turned back, she caught Julia and Anabel exchanging more looks, their eyes even wider than before.

"Which *one*?" Anabel repeated.

"There's more than one?" Julia added.

"What happened to Mr. Perfect?"

While Maggie immediately pictured Arnie and wondered how on earth they'd heard about the recent development, Aimee waved one hand and rolled her eyes. "Please," Aimee said, handing Maggie three purple highlighters and *People* magazine. "That was over months ago."

"Really?" Julia squeaked.

"The Abercrombie surfer who did crossword puzzles with his grandmother, volunteered at homeless shelters, and worshipped you?" Anabel looked at Maggie, shocked. "What *happened*?"

Maggie's heart sank slightly. She really wished it wouldn't, because everything was so good, and she was so happy now, but she couldn't help it. The last time she'd seen Julia and Anabel was in the drugstore at the beginning of the summer, right before she'd told Peter Applewood that she liked him—and learned that he didn't feel the same way. That day, in Maggie's defense and for Julia's and Anabel's benefit, Aimee had made Peter sound like Leonardo DiCaprio.

"They grew apart." Aimee shrugged. "It happens. Especially when high school guys start asking you out."

Maggie wished she could've enjoyed Julia's and Anabel's stunned disbelief, but instead, her heart sank again. It was true that Ben, her cute coworker at Camp Sound View, was in high school and had asked her out . . . but he'd also stopped talking to her the second he found out that she once ate chocolate the way other people breathe oxygen.

"And by the way," Aimee added, as though letting Julia and Anabel in on a secret, "high school guys aren't all they're cracked up to be. Which is why Maggie had to move on to someone else."

"But I'm *so* glad you had a great summer," Maggie said quickly. Julia and Anabel looked like Aimee had just told them Maggie had won $100 million in the lottery and given away every penny.

"Maybe you can tell us all about it at school next week,"

Aimee suggested. She picked up Maggie's shopping basket and handed it to her.

"Right." Maggie took the basket and started walking down the aisle. "Can't believe it—eighth grade already!"

Maggie knew Julia and Anabel were watching her and Aimee head for the register, eyes still wide and mouths open. Maybe later, once they were out of the store and out of interrogation range, she'd find the encounter funny. But right then, all she could think about was getting *out*.

Reaching the checkout, Maggie quickly unloaded her basket onto the counter. As the saleswoman rang up her school supplies, Maggie's heart sank yet again. "I forgot it."

"Impossible," Aimee said automatically. "You have enough there to educate an entire school."

"Arnie's *card*," Maggie groaned quietly. "I have to go back."

"Mags. Seriously. Send him an e-mail."

Maggie glanced over her shoulder. She knew Julia and Anabel couldn't have gotten far. And even though the last thing she wanted was to risk any unwanted questions, she also couldn't leave the store without Arnie's card.

Thinking only of him, her cute, funny, almost-first boyfriend, she left the counter and strode back toward the stationery aisle. Anabel and Julia still stood where she and Aimee had left them, whispering fiercely, but Maggie just flashed a smile and grabbed the first card she reached in the "Thinking of You" section.

Later, once safely back home and thinking more clearly, she might regret the fast selection. After all, the picture of a heart-shaped piece of chocolate under the pink-scripted "You're Sweet" was covered in silver glitter. But then again, since the inside of the card was blank, and she'd have to write out exactly what she wanted to say, she might not. Either way, she really couldn't go wrong.

Because she was giving the card to Arnie, her very first boyfriend.

Almost.

2.

"Too short." Maggie's mom shook her head.

"Too long." Aimee dumped the contents of a makeup case on the bed.

"Too black." Summer shoved a handful of popcorn in her mouth.

Maggie looked down at the skirt she wore. It hugged her hips without accenting her stomach, flowed away from her legs, and fell just above her knees. It looked great with the gray sleeveless shirt she'd bought just for the occasion. Plus, it was *black*, a color that, despite losing forty pounds, she still appreciated for its famous slimming effects.

"Whoa," Maggie's dad said from the doorway. "When'd the clouds roll in?"

"*Dad,*" Summer declared indignantly. "This is girl time."

"And dark colors are very chic and mysterious," Aimee added.

"You're right." He held up both hands, one of which held a red Netflix envelope. "I was just seeing which of my girls would be joining me for a little *Chronicles of Narnia* action."

"Did you not notice the enormous wall calendar hanging in the kitchen?" Maggie's mom asked. "The one with all the fist-size Xs counting down to a very special occasion?"

Maggie's dad gasped. "Is that *today*?" he asked innocently.

"Yes." Maggie grinned and rolled her eyes. "My very first date with Arnie is today. In half an hour, as a matter of fact."

"Well, isn't that nice," her dad said. "Arnie's a very nice boy. Very polite."

Turning slightly to see her reflection in the full-length mirror, Maggie saw her mom and Aimee exchange amused looks. Her dad did like Arnie (what wasn't to like, after all?), but when he found out that Arnie and Maggie were going on an official date, he'd made a very big deal of talking about how important *friendship* was, and how it was so nice when you could talk and laugh with someone you trusted completely, without any complications. He'd insisted that boyfriends and girlfriends come and go, but true friends are for life. Apparently, he wasn't ready for Maggie and Arnie to take their relationship to the next level.

"Okay, well, I'll let you get back to it." Her dad smiled and disappeared from the doorway—then immediately reappeared, waving the Netflix envelope. "Are you sure? Mind-blowing special effects? Based on one of the greatest children's books of all time?"

"Dad." Summer looked at him sternly, one hand in the popcorn bag. "Relax. Mom and I will watch once Maggie leaves."

"He's been holding on to *Narnia* for weeks," her mom said when her dad left the doorway again.

"It was a good plan. If any movie had a shot at keeping me here, it'd be one based on a book." Maggie crossed the room to her closet. "But, unfortunately for Dad, *no* movie has a shot. Not today."

"I think you should wear pink," Aimee suggested as Maggie began flipping through other skirts and shirts.

"Of course you do," Maggie said without turning around.

"Seriously." Aimee hopped off the bed and reached past Maggie, into the closet.

"Oh, yes." Maggie's mom nodded approvingly.

"You'll look like a princess!" Summer squealed.

Maggie eyed the pink sundress Aimee held up. Summer was eleven years old. Of course she'd think Maggie couldn't look better if she looked like Cinderella or Sleeping Beauty. But would Arnie agree?

"It's even longer than the skirt, which is a shame considering how great your legs look after being in the sun all summer, but it's *pink*." Aimee beamed. "Pink is sweet. Pink is romantic. And you look so, so pretty in it."

"Do you also want me to roll around in a bathtub of glitter?" Maggie teased.

"I think the DVD player might be broken!" Maggie's dad yelled suddenly from the living room. "Mags? Can you come check it out?"

Maggie giggled as her mom shook her head and slid off the bed.

"Your sister and I will keep him distracted." Her mom came over to kiss Maggie's forehead. "Just remember—you could wear a potato sack. Arnie already thinks you're beautiful."

Maggie felt her cheeks turn the same color as the dress. Once her mom and Summer left the room, she unzipped the black skirt and took the dress from a smiling Aimee. Because her mom was right. Arnie had seen her at her very worst—fat, sad, and hiding out in jeans and baggy hooded sweatshirts—and somehow, he'd managed to look past all that and like her anyway. She didn't need to try to look thinner for him.

But she could still try to look as pretty as possible.

Twenty-nine minutes later, Maggie stood in front of the full-length mirror. She didn't know if she looked like a princess, but she didn't think she looked half-bad, either. The soft pink looked nice against her golden tan, her lips shone and cheeks glowed (thanks to Aimee's makeup magic), and her light brown hair fell to her shoulders in soft waves. The bracelet Arnie had given her at her family's housewarming party a few weeks ago hung delicately on her wrist. "I think I'm ready," she said, unable to hold back a nervous smile.

"One last thing."

Maggie watched Aimee gently place silver flip-flops on the floor beside Maggie's bare feet.

"Instead of glitter," Aimee explained.

Maggie stepped into the flip-flops just as the doorbell rang. She looked up and caught Aimee's eye in the mirror.

"Ready, Cinderella?" Aimee whispered with a smile.

She managed a nod even though suddenly she wasn't so sure. As she grabbed her purse with Arnie's card and followed Aimee down the hallway, she wondered if this really was such a good idea. The last time she'd hung out with a boy who'd seemed to like her more than a friend, it'd ended in her pigging out on Reese's Pieces and crying in her bed. And that mini-breakdown was over a guy she'd hardly known and would probably never see again. If it didn't work with Arnie, she knew the resulting breakdown would deplete the candy supply of every store in a hundred-mile radius—and leave her without one of her very best friends. People didn't go back to being buddies after a failed attempt at romance, did they?

But maybe she was getting ahead of herself, because when she reached the living room and saw her friend and almost boyfriend standing near the front door with a bouquet of yellow daisies, every worry and concern immediately disappeared.

This was *Arnie*. And no matter what, they would be absolutely fine.

"Hi," she said, smiling shyly.

"Hi." He'd already been smiling, but the corners of his mouth reached even higher as she neared.

"Mags, he brought you *flowers*," Summer whispered loudly. "Real ones!"

If this were any day before today, or if the flowers had been for anyone else, Maggie would've playfully teased Arnie. She probably would've said something like, "What a *gentleman*!" or, "Who said chivalry's dead?" and then suggested Arnie'd been watching too many old movies. But it was today, and the flowers were for her. She'd never been given flowers before, and now that she had, she knew it was no joking matter.

"Thank you," she said, taking the bouquet from Arnie.

"Now, let's get a picture!"

Feeling her face flush, Maggie turned to see her dad whip out a digital camera. She quickly looked to her mom for help, but the best her mom could do was mouth, *I'm sorry,* and offer a sympathetic wince.

Maggie grabbed Arnie's sleeve and gently tugged him toward her. "The sooner we smile, the sooner we can go," she whispered.

"Heard that." Her dad raised the digital camera.

"I don't mind," Arnie said. "These shots will be great on the Patrol This website."

Deciding to save that debate for later, Maggie focused on holding her smile for seven flashes.

"Okay!" her mom finally intervened. "You guys should get going. You don't want to be late for your reservation."

As Arnie moved toward the front door, her mom and Summer distracted her dad by asking to see the pictures on the camera's small screen, and Maggie turned to Aimee.

"Will you be okay? Is your mom coming?"

"Don't worry about me." Aimee held out one hand. "I'll put those in water. And then I might hang around and take your dad up on the movie offer."

"Really?" Maggie handed Aimee the flowers. "We can give you a ride. I'm sure Arnie won't mind."

"That's okay, but thanks." She leaned closer to Maggie and lowered her voice. "If I stay here long enough, I might miss World War Seventeen at home."

Maggie frowned. She knew Aimee's parents had been having problems lately, and even talked about getting divorced, but she didn't know they were still engaging in battle in front of Aimee.

"Don't worry," she said again. "Just have fun!"

Careful not to squish the flowers between them, Maggie gave Aimee a quick hug.

"Curfew's nine o'clock!" her dad declared as Maggie joined Arnie by the front door.

"We'll have her home by eight fifty-nine," Arnie called back.

"Sorry about that," Maggie said once they stood alone on the front stoop. "Next time, we'll meet at the restaurant."

"You look so pretty," Arnie said before she could worry

about referring to "next time" before this time had even started.

Maggie's cheeks burned. On some level, she'd known things would be different. Arnie'd picked her up at her house before. He'd given her gifts and paid her compliments before. But now, knowing that he liked her as more than a friend, and that she felt the same way, everything felt different—somehow bigger, more important. It was almost like they'd just met, and were getting to know each other for the first time. Which wasn't bad. It would just take some getting used to.

"You look great," she finally responded. It was the truth. He always looked great, but tonight, in his khakis and white button-down shirt, he looked even better.

Things continued to feel different all the way to the restaurant. They sat together in the backseat of Arnie's parents' fancy silver SUV, and for the first time ever, she paid attention to the distance between them. Did they always sit so far apart? Did her arm always press up against the door? Did he always stare out the window? And she wondered if they were always so quiet while in the car. Was it because his family's driver drove them? And because Arnie didn't want him to relay anything they said to his parents? But didn't the driver *usually* drive them?

One thing she was sure of was that the drive lasted much longer than usual. She wasn't sure where they were going to dinner, but since they'd picked her up, she'd assumed they were staying in her neighborhood.

"Where are we *going*?" she asked a few minutes after passing Nora's, the nicest restaurant in town. The only other options were Applebee's and an assortment of other chains. Arnie wouldn't have picked any of those for their very first official date.

"You'll see." He grinned.

Nearly forty minutes after leaving her house, they finally pulled onto a long, paved driveway surrounded by forest, nowhere near anything else. They drove for about another mile, and eventually reached what looked like the kind of log cabin Donald Trump might build if he ever felt outdoorsy. It was two stories tall, had a wide, wraparound porch, and sat in the middle of what looked more like a park than a yard.

"The Lodge?" she squeaked, spotting the large wooden sign near the parking lot.

"You know it?" Arnie sounded pleased.

"Isn't this where Tom Cruise and Katie Holmes had Suri's last birthday party?"

"Built last year and dubbed by the *New York Times* as the

secluded, exclusive dining destination for the nature-loving rich and famous." He turned to her. "Like it?"

She nodded, too stunned to speak. Compared to this place, Nora's, with its pretty white Christmas lights and soft linen napkins, was probably about as fancy as Taco Bell.

Arnie got out of the car and came around to her side. She thanked his driver for the ride and took Arnie's hand when he opened the door.

If things had felt different before, now they felt like part of someone else's life. As they walked up the winding stone path to the restaurant's entrance, she took it all in—the sprawling green lawn, beds of colorful flowers, birds chirping overhead, and large, sparkling lake, visible through The Lodge's many windows—and wondered how she, boring old Maggie Bean, had gotten there.

With a *boy*.

"Gunderson, for two," Arnie said when they reached the hostess station.

They followed the hostess through a spacious lobby with huge wooden beams overhead and an enormous stone fireplace. Passing a mirror, Maggie glanced quickly to make sure her hair was okay and that her mouth didn't still hang open from shock.

"I requested to sit outside," Arnie said as they weaved

through the main dining area, which was filled with long tables that looked like slices of sanded tree trunks. "I hope that's okay."

Okay? Was he kidding?

The hostess led them outside, and across and down a series of decks.

"It's like a tree house," Maggie said in awe, once they were seated.

They had their own small square of deck, separated from a larger deck and other diners by two steps leading down. They were surrounded by green, leafy tree branches, but still had a perfect view of the lake glittering in the setting sun.

"I just wanted to make sure you would never forget it."

"It?" She looked away from the lake and at him.

He paused and focused on spreading the linen napkin in his lap. "Our first official date," he said without looking up.

She leaned across the table and waited for his eyes to meet hers. "*That* will never happen," she promised.

As she sat back, she took her linen napkin from the table. She wasn't sure if it was nervousness, excitement, or a little bit of both, but when she went to gently tug the napkin out from under the silverware, she yanked too hard and sent her utensils flying. The big fork clattered to the floor several feet away, and the little fork landed on a salad dish on the tree-house tier below theirs.

"See?" she said quickly, trying to ignore the heat spreading from her cheeks to her forehead as other diners turned toward them. "Totally unforgettable."

Thankfully, the waiter appeared right then with menus (and a new set of silverware). As Maggie opened her menu and surveyed the fish, chicken, and other low-carb options, Arnie took a sip of water—and immediately started choking.

"Arnie—"

"I'm okay," he gasped, his face turning bright red. "Just give me a sec."

Her heart raced as she watched him struggle to breathe. She was about to jump up and pound him on the back when he finally managed to inhale and exhale without coughing.

"Wrong pipe," he croaked.

Not wanting to embarrass him, she tried to turn her attention back to the menu. "Are you sure you're okay?" she asked gently when he took the napkin from his lap and blotted his damp forehead.

He nodded.

She lifted the menu so she could sneak peeks without him noticing. He looked seriously pained, like he'd choked on a pack of thumbtacks, not water.

"Maggie," he finally said, leaning toward her but looking out at the lake, "I kind of have a problem."

She lowered the menu. "Do you need an ambulance? Should we call 911?"

"Maybe." He tried to laugh, then forced himself to look at her. When he spoke again, his voice was so quiet, she had to strain to hear. "This place is *really* expensive. I knew it was, but I had no idea the cheapest thing on the menu was thirty dollars. And I kind of didn't bring enough money."

Was that all? Maggie leaned so close, their noses practically touched. "That's okay," she said. "I have money too."

He shook his head. "I don't want you to pay for anything. This was my idea."

She sat back. This wasn't the way their very first official date was supposed to go. They weren't supposed to be anything but 100 percent happy. And even though it'd felt like they were getting to know each other all over again, Maggie knew Arnie well enough to know that he wasn't going to change his mind about letting her help pay—and that he'd be mad at himself for weeks if they simply left and went somewhere else.

Catching their waiter's eye, she waved him over.

"What're you doing?" Arnie whispered nervously.

"I have an idea," she whispered back.

"Yes, miss?" The waiter smiled.

"I was just wondering," Maggie said sweetly, "if you have a children's menu?"

One hot dog, one cheeseburger, and two vanilla milk-shakes later, the sun hung low in the sky, the lake looked like it was sprinkled with sapphires, and Maggie and Arnie laughed till their sides ached—the way they always did when they were together.

3. "So, let me get this straight," Aimee said, taking a stack of notebooks from Maggie. "You gave him the card, he said it was the best thing he's ever gotten in his entire life . . . and no kiss?"

Maggie nodded. "That about covers it."

Aimee tossed the notebooks in her locker and turned to Maggie. "Peck on the cheek?"

"Nope."

"On your hand?"

"Negative."

"On your forehead?"

"*Nada.*"

"Huh." Aimee took a handful of pencils from Maggie and casually threw them on top of the notebooks. "That doesn't make any sense."

Maggie shrugged. "I guess it just wasn't the right time." That, or she'd said or done something at some point during her first official date with Arnie to make him change his mind about her. She didn't suggest this to Aimee, though, since she'd already replayed every single perfect moment in her mind and still had no idea where things could've gone wrong.

"Weird."

"You know what else doesn't make sense?" Maggie asked, hoping to change the subject.

"There's more?" Aimee looked at Maggie, then followed Maggie's gaze to her locker. "What?"

"If you just throw everything in there without any kind of organization, how are you ever going to find anything?"

Aimee turned back to Maggie. "Really? You really want to go there?"

"I'm looking out for you."

"You're living vicariously through my locker since you're too chicken to go to your own."

"I'm not chicken," Maggie said defensively. "I just haven't had the chance to go down that hall yet."

"Mags, talk about not making sense. It's the first day of school. You *love* the first day of school. It's like Christmas, for you."

"So?"

"*So*, opening your locker is like opening Christmas presents, a joyous experience you look forward to for weeks. And you keep coming to my locker instead of going to your own."

Maggie glanced around. When she was sure no one was paying attention, she leaned toward Aimee. "I can't do it," she admitted. "I thought it'd be a piece of cake. I've seen him at least five times since telling him I like him and getting a big 'no thanks' in return, and it's been fine. But this is different. It's just us—alone, again, at our lockers. You know what that means."

"What that *meant*," Aimee said. "Seeing Peter Applewood at your locker this year won't be like it was last year. A lot's happened since then."

She was right. Maggie *knew* she was right. They could just say hi, ask which class they had or were about to go to, and pretend like nothing had ever happened. Like Maggie had never looked forward to seeing him every forty-five minutes every day, or that she'd never confessed how she felt, or that he'd never rejected her. They could just start over. They could just be friends.

Starting after next period.

"Saved by the bell," Aimee said as the ringing sounded overhead and classmates started to scatter.

Maggie's backpack was already heavy after collecting textbooks in the first three classes of the day, so she shrugged it off her shoulders and held it by the straps.

"This is eighth grade," Aimee reminded her as they headed down the hallway. "There are going to be *lots* of books. You're not going to carry that backpack around like that all year."

"Just think of all the muscles I'm working," Maggie quipped. "By the end of the year, I'll be so buff, you won't even recognize me."

"Speaking of that . . ."

Maggie stopped short to keep from running into Aimee, who'd frozen in the gymnasium doorway.

"Ms. *Pinkerton?*" Maggie said when she realized what Aimee was talking about. It was out of her mouth before she could stop it.

The cranky gym teacher glanced up from her clipboard and glared at Maggie from underneath her faded Yankees baseball cap. "What? You need an engraved invitation, Bean?"

Knowing Ms. Pinkerton well enough to know that answering would only give her more reason to grumble, Maggie hooked one arm through Aimee's and headed for the bleachers.

"What *happened*?" Aimee whispered once they were sitting down.

"Major identity crisis," a voice whispered back. "Caused by a bad breakup."

Maggie turned around to see where the inside scoop was coming from. Too distracted by Ms. Pinkerton to pay attention to where they were sitting, Maggie and Aimee had plopped down only two rows in front of Julia and Anabel.

"Rumor has it she thought she was getting engaged at the beginning of the summer," Julia continued quietly, blue eyes glittering, "but then all she got was a big old broken heart."

"Oh, *no*," Aimee said, frowning. "Poor Ms. P!"

Maggie turned back, her mind racing. Julia Swanson was actually initiating conversation with her and Aimee in gym class, something that never, *ever* would've happened last year, and Ms. Pinkerton looked like she'd spent the summer reading fashion magazines and trying—unsuccessfully—to implement their hip wardrobe tips. Ms. Pinkerton had always worn baggy shorts, T-shirts, and sneakers, rather masculine ensembles that had caused her to be mistaken for the boys' gym teacher on more than one occasion. But today, she was wearing skintight purple leggings, a bright green caftan . . . and gold high heels. The mismatched outfit was so feminine, if it weren't for the faded Yankees baseball hat, Maggie would've thought Ms. Pinkerton was someone else.

Not that her new look affected her old charm.

"Vacation's over, people!" she bellowed suddenly from the gymnasium floor. "Stop wandering around like a bunch of lazy tourists and take a seat!"

"They were supposedly together for a *decade*," Julia hissed behind Maggie and Aimee as other classmates took to the bleachers. "Ms. Pinkerton thought she was getting a ring for their ten-year anniversary, and instead all she got was *Lost* on DVD. She was so devastated, she immediately tried to turn herself into the kind of person she thought he wanted her to be."

"A more feminine fashion disaster?" Aimee peered over her shoulder. "And how do you know all this?"

Maggie glanced back to see Julia shrug smugly.

"My mom," she said.

Maggie and Aimee nodded. That wasn't surprising. The only person who spent more time at Water Wings practices than the Water Wings themselves was Mrs. Swanson, and not because she especially loved being class cheerleader. Julia's mom loved her daughter. But she loved gossiping even more.

"Okay, ladies!"

Maggie turned back to see Ms. Pinkerton standing at the bottom of the bleachers.

"We have a few things to go over," she continued, wincing as she shifted from one gold high heel to the other. "First order of business—your gym uniform. If it ain't broke, we're not fixing it."

Maggie was so distracted by Ms. Pinkerton's appearance, she hardly heard the speech. Not only did Ms. Pinkerton look like she was trying out some sort of glamour-girl Halloween costume a few weeks early, she'd also gone so far as to do her hair and makeup. Maggie didn't wear much makeup, but she knew enough about it to know that "less is more" was usually the way to go. Unfortunately, no one had shared this tip with Ms. Pinkerton; her cheeks were flaming red, her lips were magenta and outlined in purple, and her eyelids were bright green. And instead of the usual ponytail sticking out from the back of the baseball cap, Ms. Pinkerton's hair hung in tight curls—not pretty, loose waves—to her shoulders. She looked like she was trying *really* hard . . . which was almost worse than looking like she wasn't trying at all.

"Last order of business!" Ms. Pinkerton declared, snapping Maggie from her appearance analysis. "In the locker room are sign-up sheets for every athletic team and club meeting this fall. You snooze, you lose, so if you have any interest in participating, you'd better sign up now."

Maggie heaved her backpack onto her shoulders and stood, happy to have a reason to visit the sports sign-up table for the first time ever.

"One more thing!" Ms. Pinkerton shouted over the din of papers shuffling and bleachers squeaking.

"Do you want to put some of your books in my bag?"

Maggie glanced up to see Julia and Anabel standing right behind her and Aimee. Anabel's half-empty backpack hung from one shoulder, partially unzipped.

"Your backpack looks like it might rip at the seams, and I have plenty of room."

She didn't seem to be kidding. Maggie was debating whether to take her up on the offer—if not to reciprocate the attempt at civility, then to ease the dull pain that already throbbed in her back—but before she could respond, two shrill whistles sounded from below.

"Listen up!" Ms. Pinkerton hollered. "Due to current school budget concerns, some extracurricular activities are being evaluated. Which means that some teams that were offered last year might be cut this year."

Maggie looked at Aimee.

"More specifically," Ms. Pinkerton continued, "if you

plan to sign up for either the synchronized or regular swim team, go ahead, but don't bust out the bathing suit just yet. Pool maintenance is pricey, and one of those teams will go."

Maggie's chin dropped against her neck. After training for Water Wings tryouts and sinking into the worst candy depression she'd ever known when she didn't make it, the swim team had changed her life. It had made her stronger, thinner, and healthier. Regardless of how things had turned out with Peter Applewood, swimming had given her the confidence to reveal her feelings in the first place, which had eventually led to becoming Arnie's almost-first girlfriend. Swimming had gotten her into good enough shape to, she hoped, run the annual mile in gym class without stopping once to catch her breath.

She felt better in the pool than she did anywhere else, and had looked forward to practicing with the team all summer.

Maggie looked up just in time to see Anabel and Julia, Water Wings cocaptains, exchange shocked looks. Careful to avoid making eye contact with Maggie, Anabel zipped up her half-empty backpack and shifted it to her other shoulder.

"Wait till I tell my mother," Julia declared before taking Anabel's elbow and stomping down the bleachers.

4. "They don't seem very excited, do they?" Arnie asked.

"Can you blame them?" Maggie looked out to the crowd of kids gathering in the classroom. "Last week they were sleeping late and playing video games. This week they're getting up early for school and being dragged to weight-loss meetings. That's a pretty painful double-whammy."

He turned to her and grinned. "Little do they know that after sixty fun-filled minutes with the Patrol This dream team, the only thing they'll want to do with that video game controller is use it as a weight for bicep curls."

"Will that be the next edition of Arnie the Abdominator?" Maggie asked, grateful for a reason to turn toward the projector screen hanging on the wall behind them. Two weeks ago, when they were still just friends, hearing him refer to them as a "dream team" would've made her smile. Now, it made her cheeks turn pink. She wanted Arnie to know she liked him, but she wasn't sure she wanted him to know that she liked him so much that even the *idea* of the two of them being any kind of team made her blush.

"Did you see the last one?" Arnie's voice was excited as he looked at the Patrol This website home page blown up on the projector screen. His smiling face sat on top of a young Arnold Schwarzenegger's muscular body in the bottom-right-hand corner.

"Yes," Maggie said as Arnie clicked on Arnold's shiny chest and a video of him holding on to the back of his living room couch and rolling from side to side on his skateboard appeared. "I did it for twenty minutes and was sore for three days."

"But I bet you didn't you notice how hard you were working while you were doing it, right?"

"Right." He sounded so pleased with himself, she couldn't help but smile.

"And why's that?" he prodded lightly.

"Because," she said, rolling her eyes playfully when he turned back to her, "the Abdominator knows how to pump you up."

He frowned.

She looked at him. "There are no known exercises to shrink a big head, you know."

"It's not about me," he said seriously. "Or about my ego. It's about branding. And marketing our product. Who's going to sign up for the Abdominator e-mail newsletter if I don't sound as cool and powerful as possible at all times?"

"Fine." She forced the smile from her face and took a deep breath. When she spoke again, she sounded like a teenage boy from a faraway country. "Arnie the Abdominator knows how to pump *you* up."

"Awesome." He grinned and quickly squeezed her hand "Thank you."

She opened her mouth to say "you're welcome," but nothing came out. The words got lost somewhere in her swirling head as soon as his fingers touched hers.

"Can you believe it?"

"No," Maggie said automatically, even though she guessed Electra probably wasn't talking about the strange effects being so close to Arnie was now having on her.

"We're up to fifteen kids. *Fifteen.* That's almost double our last session." Electra stood between Maggie and Arnie and put one arm around each of them. "I'm so happy word's getting out."

"Speaking of happy," Arnie said, "where's the sparkly asparagus? The glittery orange?"

"The coloring books and crayons?" Maggie added, suppressing a giggle. As the beloved leader of Pound Patrollers, Electra was great at helping grown-ups lose weight, but her success there hadn't quite translated to Patrol This, which had been formed by the Pound Patrollers organization for kids even younger than Maggie and Arnie. The first and only other time they'd started a Patrol This session, Electra had dressed up as a spandex-clad superhero, festooned the classroom in enormous cardboard cutouts of fruits and vegetables, and placed coloring books about grocery shopping on every desk. There'd been glaring reminders everywhere of why the kids were there—and as any chubby kid knows, reminders that you're chubby are *never* necessary. It had taken all of five minutes for Arnie to intervene, and after that first good-intentioned misstep, he and Maggie had led most of the meetings.

"Hey." Electra gently hip-checked Arnie, then Maggie. "You live, you learn. This time I'm sticking with the adults and leaving the kids to those who know best."

"You won't be disappointed," Arnie assured her. "Maggie and I have been spending a lot of time together—"

"In a completely and totally professional way, of

course." Maggie shrugged when Arnie leaned forward and raised his eyebrows at her. She didn't want their new personal relationship to affect their old working relationship, or for Electra to think that they wouldn't continue to take their Patrol This responsibilities just as seriously as they always had.

"Excuse me . . . ?"

Electra stepped toward a puzzled-looking mother holding the hand of a scowling little boy.

"I'm sorry to interrupt," the mother said, wincing and tightening her grip on her son's hand when he tried to yank it away, "but we're looking for Patrol This?"

"You've found it," Electra said. "I'm Electra, and this is Arnie and Maggie, our weight-loss dream team."

Maggie looked down when the heat in her cheeks instantly flared up again.

"May I show you to your seats?" Electra reached one arm forward to usher the mother and her son to an empty pair of desks, and then shot Arnie and Maggie a pointed look over her shoulder.

"If we can make *him* smile by the end of the meeting, we're miracle workers," Maggie whispered, watching the little boy stomp his feet and refuse to sit down.

"Miracle workers, huh?" Arnie seemed to consider this

as he looked back to the screen behind them. "I wonder if the website people could fit that in somewhere. . . ."

"Welcome, everyone!"

Maggie's heart fluttered in her chest as she turned away from the screen and joined Electra by the front desk. Like Arnie, she felt pretty good about what they had planned for the kids, but she was still nervous. Their first session had gone so well, the Pound Patrollers corporate office had given Arnie and Maggie cash bonuses and asked them to continue to help with the program. And while that vote of confidence had made Arnie even more comfortable leading the kids, it had done the opposite for Maggie. Last time, there were no expectations. This time, real businesspeople had invested actual money in them.

Plus, as Electra had pointed out, now there were *fifteen* kids to inspire and encourage. And judging by the latecomers trickling into the classroom, that number was only going to grow.

Maggie smiled and scanned the room as Electra introduced her, Arnie, and the program. The parents listened attentively and nodded. Every now and then a mother nudged her daughter or patted her son's back, as if the kids were making the same connections at the same time instead of pouting, staring off into space, or picking at their fingernails. The last little boy who came in sat slumped in his chair with his arms crossed over his chest, and glared at the desk the entire time Electra spoke. He probably would've eventually slid all the way to the floor in protest, but, thankfully, Electra kept the introduction short.

"Hi, guys," Arnie said easily once Electra sat down in a metal folding chair on the side of the classroom. "How's it going?"

The parents had stopped nodding and now looked skeptical. A few of the kids looked up curiously, but most didn't even seem to hear him.

"Everyone happy to be back in school?"

Maggie glanced at Arnie when no one answered.

"Well, I'm not." Arnie leaned against the front desk. "I had a great summer—no, an *amazing* summer. Probably the best summer of my entire life."

Maggie looked down at her sneakers when the pink in her cheeks spread to her nose, chin, and forehead. She wondered if it had been the best summer of Arnie's entire life for the same reason it had been the best summer of her entire life: because by the end of it, they were together.

"It's always hard going back to homework and tests and papers after three months of freedom," Arnie continued. "I mean, who likes giving that up to sit at a desk and listen to teachers rattle on about whatever *they* think is important for hours every day?"

"Not me!"

Maggie bit back a smile when the boy yelled from his seat in the back of the classroom. His mother looked mortified, but he looked interested for the first time since entering the room.

"Me neither," a little girl agreed.

"We have *lives*," another boy chimed in. "They don't think so, but we do."

"I know you do," Arnie said. He sounded as serious as they did. "So do I. So does Maggie. And believe me—the teachers don't stop rambling once you hit eighth grade. If anything, they start talking even more."

A few of the mothers exchanged concerned looks as the kids groaned.

"And it's been really tough getting back into this year, especially after having the best summer ever." He paused. "But you know what helps?"

"Video games?" a little boy guessed.

"Movies?" another offered.

"Counting down to Christmas vacation?" a third asked.

"All very good distractions," Arnie agreed. "But even better, at least for me, is talking to kids who are going through the same exact thing."

"But you can't talk while the teacher's talking," a cute girl with curly brown hair pointed out. "It's not allowed."

"You're absolutely right. Talking while the teacher's talking probably isn't a good idea. But talking after class is definitely a good idea."

"Like . . . in a club?" a girl with long blond hair suggested.

"Exactly." Arnie grinned.

"We don't have clubs," the blonde said.

"We're too young," the Christmas vacation boy explained.

"You're not too young for this one," Arnie said.

"This isn't a club," a boy with dark hair and deep dimples declared. "Or, if it is, it's for our *parents.*"

Arnie waved his hand, as if to say adults weren't his concern. "Your parents have each other. And now *we*"—he pointed to himself, Maggie, and half a dozen kids throughout the room—"have each other. This is *our* club. We're going to have a lot of fun, and we can talk about anything we want every time we get together."

"Even our parents?" the Christmas vacation boy asked coyly, grinning at his mother.

"Absolutely," Arnie said. "The only limit we have is time—because we *do* have lives, and so we only get to meet for an hour each week."

Maggie smiled. The parents still looked uncertain, but the kids were hooked. This was part of the plan, and what had made their first session so successful. Arnie spoke to the kids like he was one of them—which he was. He didn't talk down to them or make them feel like they were there because they'd done something wrong. They responded to that, and came to trust him—and the program—much faster than they would if he'd immediately started lecturing them on calories, sugar, and refined carbohydrates. Those might've been the things that interested adults—but Patrol This wasn't for adults.

"Now, I hope you don't mind if I start things off," Arnie continued with a big sigh, "but I have a problem that I've been *dying* to talk to someone about all week. Cafeteria food. How am I supposed to stay healthy when my only options are grilled cheese, tater tots, and pizza? How is that fair? Who on earth makes those menu decisions?"

"And the *cookies*?" Maggie added. "They just give them to you without even asking. Sugar cookies, chocolate chip cookies, oatmeal raisin cookies . . . a different kind every day."

"Don't forget the ice cream!"

Maggie grinned. The scowling boy who'd stomped his feet while refusing to sit down was not only sitting straight up in his chair—he was participating. His mother looked stunned.

A sudden movement made Maggie look toward the back of the room. When she did, her grin dropped slightly, and froze. She'd been so caught up in what Arnie was saying—or perhaps just in Arnie himself—that she hadn't noticed anyone else come into the room. Five more kids and their parents listened while standing, because all of the desks and chairs were already taken.

Which meant there were now *twenty* kids to inspire and encourage. That was almost three times as many as they had in their first session. Maggie didn't know if they could pull it off . . . but if they did, they just might have to add "Arnie and Maggie, Miracle Workers" under their pictures on the Patrol This website.

5. "Take a wrong turn in the locker room, Bean?"

"Sorry," Maggie said breathlessly. She shuffled as fast as her weighted-down feet would carry her toward the bleachers, where the rest of the swim team already sat. "I had to talk to my English teacher, stop by the French club office, drop off some papers to—"

Ms. Pinkerton fired a quick, short breath into her whistle. "Do you think I just sit around twiddling my thumbs and counting down the minutes until I get to see you people?"

"No?" Maggie guessed, trying not to gawk at Ms. Pinkerton's latest style shocker: a short denim skirt, a tight pink T-shirt under an orange sweater vest, and furry black boots.

Ms. Pinkerton frowned. "We all have things, Bean, yet everyone but you managed to get here on time."

"I'm sorry." Maggie slowed down and dropped onto the bleacher seat like she'd also climbed Mount Everest after talking to her English teacher, stopping by the French Club office, and dropping off papers to the Mathletes coordinator. She was now eleven days into eighth grade and still hadn't been to her locker to drop off any books. Her backpack was so heavy, sometimes she carried it in front of her and supported the bottom with both arms to keep it from ripping. "It won't happen again."

"You're right. It won't. Especially not if there are no more meetings to attend because the swim team no longer exists."

Maggie sat up straight, immediately forgetting the throbbing in her shoulders and back. Quickly scanning the bleachers behind her, she grew even more nervous when she saw her fellow swim team members' serious expressions.

"Now, as I was saying," Ms. Pinkerton continued, slowly pacing in front of them, "it's not looking good. Under normal circumstances, our first meeting of the season would be used to review last year's accomplishments and strategize for maximum success and district domination this year. But these aren't normal circumstances."

"Ms. P," Maggie said tentatively, raising her hand. "What

exactly is going on? The swim team and Water Wings have shared the pool for years. What's changed?"

Ms. Pinkerton stopped pacing and looked across the room as the group of girls gathered in a large circle near the far end of the pool burst into shrill giggles. Her eyes narrowed as Julia Swanson and Anabel Richards made their way around the inside edge of the circle, handing a pink long-stemmed rose to each Water Wings member.

"Those flowers must've cost at least fifty dollars." Ms. Pinkerton crossed her arms over her chest and shook her head.

"Did we, like, run out of money?" Shasta Lorne, another eighth grader and the team's 100-meter butterfly record holder, asked worriedly.

"Or do something wrong?" added Kim Wu, a seventh grader and their best relay closer.

Ms. Pinkerton's head snapped toward them. "Absolutely not. We've done everything we're supposed to. These bleachers are packed with spectators every time we have a home meet. We sell wrapping paper until everyone we know has enough shiny packaging for twenty years' worth of Christmas and birthday gifts. We use that profit to pay for our uniforms and gear, and whatever's left over we donate to the YMCA in town. We give, give, give, and we never ask for anything in return."

"So then . . . why?" Maggie didn't want to make Ms. Pinkerton more upset than she already was, but she also didn't want her storming out in a huff before saying what was really going on.

As Ms. Pinkerton resumed pacing, her furry black boots reminded Maggie of fluffy little dogs. "See that kid dozing off in his high chair over there?"

Maggie and her teammates looked toward the lifeguard stand. The guard was slouched over his rescue tube, twirling his whistle cord around one finger and staring at the wall clock on the other side of the pool. Every now and then he blinked suddenly and lifted his head, like he'd started to fall asleep before remembering that he wasn't home in bed.

"Guess how much that supposedly CPR-certified and exceptionally skilled life preserver makes an hour."

"Ten dollars?" Maggie offered. She'd made about that much as a junior swim instructor at Camp Sound View over the summer.

Ms. Pinkerton snorted. "If that were true, you'd all be wearing gold goggles rimmed with diamonds."

"Twenty?" Shasta suggested.

"The goggles would be silver, but you'd still get the rocks." Ms. Pinkerton stopped walking, clasped her hands behind her back, and faced them. "Fifty."

Maggie's mouth dropped open as her teammates gasped.

"Think about it. In season, the girl's swim team meets for two hours every day, five days a week. That means every week the school's paying Lazy Larry—"

"Five hundred dollars," Maggie said, calculating quickly.

Ms. Pinkerton paused, letting the number sink in. "And that's just for us. The Water Wings *also* meet for two hours every day, five days a week. They usually meet after we do, which means Lazy Lamont, Lazy Larry's lifeguard friend, gets another five hundred dollars. That's a *thousand dollars* every week."

"Can't they trade in Lamont and Larry for cheaper lifeguards?" Shasta asked.

"I'll do it for forty," Kim quipped.

"No, they can't hire cheaper lifeguards," Ms. Pinkerton said, ignoring Kim's offer. "There are rules. What if one of you smiles a little too wide while thinking of your boyfriend underwater and starts choking? Someone slightly more qualified than Ms. Hu will have to clear your lungs and save your life."

Maggie looked down, suddenly very interested in her backpack zipper. Lately, she'd found herself thinking of Arnie at all sorts of strange times—while brushing her teeth, or chasing Summer to the TV remote control, or reading *A Tale of Two Cities* before bed. That was on top of all the other thinking about him she did during the times she expected to think about him, like when they were on the phone, or while her mom was driving her to and from Patrol This, or every time she looked at the silver bracelet with the aquamarine stone on her wrist. She'd always thought of only one thing while swimming during practice and meets, and that was to move as far as possible, as fast as possible. Would unexpected thoughts of Arnie surprise her underwater—and slow her down?

"And the lifeguard situation is only part of the problem," Ms. Pinkerton continued. "Keeping a pool up and running is very expensive. Everything in and around it costs money—the water, lights, maintenance. And then there are the extra costs associated with it being a school pool, like custodial services and after-hours security. Unfortunately, the school's wallet has slowly been growing thinner, and this year, it's just about empty."

"Can't we share the pool?" Maggie asked amid groans. It wasn't an ideal solution—the swim team and Water Wings didn't exactly coexist harmoniously—but swimming near them had to be better than not swimming at all.

"Brilliant suggestion, Bean."

Maggie smiled.

"And the board already thought of it."

Maggie's smile faded.

"As you know, the pool has always been shared—we split it with the boys' swim team, and the Water Wings split it with water polo. But now there will only be one girls' team sharing with one boys' team, for one two-hour session every day."

"So either the boys' swim team or the water polo team has to go too?" Shasta asked.

"Yes," Ms. Pinkerton said. "And since boys are genetically predisposed to be more immature and illogical than girls, they'll probably duke it out with fists and fury. I hope we can be a bit more civilized."

"What do we have to do?" Kim asked.

"And how much time do we have?" Shasta added.

"We have four weeks," Ms. Pinkerton said. "At the end of the month, the school board wants representatives from every team to make a presentation. Based on those, they will decide who stays and who goes."

"That's not fair!" Maggie declared.

Ms. Pinkerton looked at Maggie with a combination of amusement and annoyance by the outburst.

"I'm sorry," Maggie said. "Or, no—I'm not. Because it *isn't* fair. You know it. We know it. And they definitely know it."

"They *are* kind of acting like they've already won," Kim said glumly when Maggie nodded to the Water Wings.

"How can they be *laughing* at a time like this?" Shasta marveled.

It was true. While Maggie and the swim team members were stressing about whether they would ever get to do what they loved to do again, the Water Wings were talking, smelling their pink roses, and laughing every time Anabel and Julia spoke. They looked like they were just killing time until given the green light to put on their signature silver swimsuits and dive on in.

"The Water Wings always get what they want," Maggie said. "Everyone loves them. All of our teachers think they're so pretty, and sweet, and talented. It would be one thing if we were deciding among ourselves, or even flipping a coin . . . but if the school board is making the call, we don't stand a chance."

"Wrong, Bean," Ms. Pinkerton said gruffly, stepping toward her. "Not everyone loves them."

Maggie leaned back and looked up. Ms. Pinkerton stood so close, Maggie could see clumps of black mascara gluing her eyelashes together.

"You work hard," Ms. Pinkerton said. "You *all* work hard. Yes, you can be whiny, and bratty, and downright intolerable. But you focus when it matters. You pull it out when it counts. And for that reason, I think you deserve to be in that pool more than anyone." She squared her shoulders and stepped back. "And we're going to make it impossible for them to say no."

"How do we do that?" Kim asked.

"We do what every great and successful group has done throughout time." Ms. Pinkerton's eyes traveled slowly across the bleachers. "We pick a leader."

"That's easy," Shasta said lightly. "No one can say no to Ms. P!"

"Probably the smartest thing to ever come out of your mouth, Lorne." Ms. Pinkerton shook her head. "But I'm not an option. The board wants to hear from ankle-biters only."

Maggie mentally reviewed the team roster. Shasta was likable but flighty. Kim was solid underwater, but cracked like an egg at the first sign of pressure on land. Jessica Phillips was smart but disorganized. Anna Shay was organized but forgetful. Libby Bernard remembered everything, but could be unintentionally condescending. Samantha Jack was great with adults, but not so much with her peers. Amelia Gregory was smart and organized, but shook like a leaf in the spotlight.

Maggie's brain lingered on Amelia. Maybe they could

work on her public speaking. They could have trial presentations—maybe start her out in front of one or two people, and build from there. After a month of training, speaking in front of the school board would be a piece of cake.

Maggie looked up to suggest Amelia—and her eyes locked on Ms. Pinkerton's. She'd been so busy silently choosing a candidate, she hadn't noticed everyone grow quiet, or Ms. Pinkerton watching her. "What?"

"Don't ask me." Ms. Pinkerton nodded toward the bleachers behind Maggie.

Maggie turned slowly in her seat, the pink in her cheeks slowly deepening to maroon. Shasta, Kim, Jessica, Anna, Libby, Samantha, Amelia, and the rest of her teammates were looking at her and smiling.

"What?" she asked again, even though she already had a pretty good idea.

"You have to do it," Shasta said, her green eyes glittering.

"*Have* to," Kim seconded.

"You're the only one who can," Anna added.

Maggie shook her head. "No. No way. I'm sorry—I care about our team and will do just about anything else to help. But not this."

"But, you've done it before," Libby said. "You've gone up against those vultures and won."

"Won?" Maggie repeated.

"They didn't want you on the team," Samantha said, "but the judges did. After you stood up to them, you had an open invite. And *you* turned *them* down to join our team instead."

"It can be like last year all over again," Shasta said excitedly. "Except this time, you can finally get the ultimate revenge."

Like last year all over again. . . .

There were parts of last year that hadn't been entirely, excruciatingly painful—like meeting Arnie, becoming good friends with Peter, and joining the swim team—but the rest of it was better left in the past. The battle with Anabel and Julia had been long and embarrassing, and Maggie had no desire to ever engage in Water Wings War II. She knew they would never be friends, but she was perfectly content with not being bitter enemies.

Maggie turned away from her beaming, expectant teammates and looked at the pool. A lot had happened because of that pool. She'd become a stronger, more confident person, and wouldn't be who she was today without it. All summer long she'd counted down the days until she could jump back in, start swimming, and feel her arms and legs cutting through the cool, clear water. And now she might never have the chance to swim there again.

She didn't need the ultimate revenge. This wasn't about giving the Water Wings what they had coming. It was about keeping what she deserved—what she'd *earned*. And, even more importantly, it was about making sure the Water Wings didn't take away the chance to become a stronger, more confident person from anyone else.

"Okay," she said finally, just as Anabel said something that made the rest of the Water Wings howl. "I'll do it."

6. "What do you know about memory?" Maggie asked, holding the cordless phone between her chin and shoulder to free her hands for typing.

"That it makes great, unforgettable memories," Arnie said on the other end of the phone. "Like all the ones I have of you."

"That you should enjoy it while you're young," her dad added, oblivious to Arnie's response—and to her smile stretching from one ear to the other. He stood in the middle of the living room and circled slowly. "Now, let me see . . . where did I put that bowl of popcorn?"

"I think he's officially lost it," Maggie whispered into the phone. She eyed the puffy yellow mountain over the top of her laptop screen. Besides the TV, it was the tallest thing in the room, and couldn't be missed. "You mean *that* bowl of popcorn?"

Her dad kept turning until he faced the coffee table. "*There* it is!" He grabbed a handful of popcorn, tossed a few kernels in his mouth, and smiled at Maggie. "See?"

"I'm serious." Maggie shook her head when he held the bowl toward her, and then returned her attention to the laptop screen. "I have a lot of work to do, and I don't know if my computer can handle it."

"Handle what?" her mom asked, coming into the living room with enough blankets to warm an entire Alaskan village.

"My life," Maggie said with a sigh.

"Should I let you go?" Arnie asked, his voice concerned.

"No," Maggie said quickly. "I can talk and type at the same time."

"How are you that busy already?" Summer dropped onto the couch next to Maggie. "We haven't even been back at school two weeks."

Maggie turned the laptop so Summer could see the screen.

"I think that's us . . . but I don't see our faces."

"Exactly." Maggie turned the laptop back. Her desktop was so cluttered with saved documents, all that was visible in the wallpaper photo of her, Summer, and their mom squeezed into a hammock was their bare feet dangling over the sides.

"I'll get it," her dad said when the doorbell rang.

As her dad headed for the door and Arnie started telling her about his latest parental drama, Maggie clicked on the Excel spreadsheet icon in the top-right corner of the computer screen. Maggie's Master Multi-Tasker, which she'd originally started to keep track of homework assignments, grades, and other short- and long-term academic goals, had expanded quite a bit in the past year, and was now bigger than ever.

In addition to several others devoted to school, there was a spreadsheet for homework, which she'd just updated with an assignment to read fifty pages of *Little Women* and a study plan for her science test next week. There was a spreadsheet for her weight, which she'd started back when she was trying to lose some and which she still maintained to make sure she didn't regain any. She'd weighed herself and recorded the scale's reading over the weekend, and was happy to see the column of 146s growing longer. There was a spreadsheet for Patrol This, which kept track of meetings, website updates, and possible blog topics. This spreadsheet was in addition to an entire separate Patrol This folder, which contained meeting agendas, activity ideas, and information about the kids. There were two spreadsheets for the swim team: one to track her swims and times, and the other to record her progress in saving the team. The latter page was alarmingly blank, since she had no idea how or where to even *begin* to save the team.

The last spreadsheet was a relatively new addition, and one she updated several times a week. After neglecting some of the most important people in her life over the summer, she'd added "MB VIPs" to make sure she didn't leave anything—or anyone—out, no matter how busy she was.

It was a lot to keep track of, but definitely worth it—so long as her computer didn't crash from the stress.

"So Dad said Mom needed to chill, and then Mom said Dad needed to get a clue, and the whole thing was just ridiculous."

"I bet," Maggie said, trying hard to hear everything Arnie said as she checked her "VIP" spreadsheet. She had Family Fun from six to seven, Aimee from seven to eight, and homework from eight to ten. Whoever was at the door wasn't there for her.

"Hey, Mags."

Maggie looked up. "Aimee?"

"Should I call back?" Arnie asked.

"No," Maggie said automatically. This was their scheduled phone time. She'd looked forward to it all day.

Aimee stood in the living room doorway and offered a small smile. "Sorry, I know I'm a little early."

"Don't be silly!" Her mother took a white fleece blanket from the pile of extras at the end of the couch, hurried across the room, and wrapped the blanket around Aimee's shoulders. "We were just getting ready for a little friendly game show competition. You can be on my team for *Wheel of Fortune*."

"And then you can switch over to mine for *Jeopardy!*," her dad added. "If I can't remember where I put the popcorn when it's right in front of my face, there's no way my brain has any room for European bodies of water or Nobel Prize winners."

Maggie rolled her eyes playfully when her dad winked at her. It was hard to believe that this time a year ago he was so down about losing his job that he'd had a hard time even getting off the couch. Back then, they lived in a smaller house and had trouble paying rent. Now, her dad was a senior project manager at Ocean Vista Pools, and they had a beautiful home of their own.

"Thanks, Mr. and Mrs. Bean," Aimee said. "But, actually,

I was hoping maybe Maggie and I could talk about some very important business."

"Business?" Maggie looked at the spiral notebook tucked under Aimee's arm.

"Yes." Aimee's voice was excited as she stepped into the living room. "I know this is Family Fun time, but I just couldn't wait to talk to you. Do you mind if we go over a few things? I promise it won't take long."

"Sure," Maggie said. As she saved the Multi-Tasker and closed the laptop, she tried to shuffle the schedule in her head. Maybe she could shorten her homework time to squeeze in some family fun before bed, and then get up half an hour early in the morning to finish her assignments. Or maybe she could keep the times the same, but read and study in the living room instead of her bedroom so she could visit with her family between subjects. Or maybe Aimee would leave earlier than originally planned, since she'd come over earlier than originally planned, and then Maggie could just swap the Aimee and Family Fun times.

"Maggie?"

Arnie. He was still waiting patiently on the phone. "I'm so sorry," she said quickly, putting her laptop on the coffee table and jumping up. "Can I call you in a little while?"

"Of course," he said. "Take your time."

Even though her carefully planned schedule had just been thrown off, Maggie couldn't keep from grinning as she followed Aimee down the hallway. Arnie had to be the sweetest, most understanding boy ever, and that made her the luckiest *girl* ever.

"Feel free to join us for sugar-free hot chocolate and home-made granola bars later," Maggie's mom called after them.

"Homemade granola bars?" Aimee asked once they were in Maggie's bedroom with the door closed.

"I know," Maggie said, kicking off her sneakers and climbing on the bed. "She's been like a health-conscious Betty Crocker ever since we moved here. She probably grew the oats herself."

"That must be nice."

Maggie watched Aimee's face as she sat cross-legged at the foot of the bed. Judging by her fleeting frown and the way her normally sparkly turquoise eyes turned down, it was clear Aimee wasn't in a joking mood.

"Aim," Maggie said gently. "You okay?"

"No."

Maggie's pulse quickened. She'd answered so quickly, something big was definitely up. "What's wrong?"

Aimee placed her notebook on the bed, opened it, and flipped past the first few pages. When she reached the page she wanted, she took a pen from behind one ear, a freshly sharpened pencil from behind the other, and a blue highlighter from her jeans pocket, then placed them neatly on the bed, next to the notebook.

Maggie stared at the writing instruments like they were weapons. It wasn't unusual to see them on her bed—she had a few ink stains on the other side of her comforter to prove it—but it was extremely unusual to see them on her bed next to Aimee.

"What's *wrong*," Aimee said, her voice serious, "is that they're trying to do it again."

Aimee looked at Maggie like she should know immediately who "they" were. "Who?" Maggie asked when she couldn't figure it out.

"*Them,*" Aimee said.

Maggie shook her head as her mind came up blank. Nobody had ever done anything to Aimee. She was too friendly, too well liked.

"The breath-holding bloodsuckers."

Maggie's eyes widened. There were few people Aimee ever spoke negatively about, and when she spoke of them, her comments were usually much tamer and along the lines of "*Someone* must be having a bad day."

"Anabel. Julia. The circle of floating floozies."

"Oh." Maggie nodded thoughtfully. "Floating floozies . . . I like it. Maybe they can get that printed on their shiny new swim caps after they've won over the board."

"Mags, that's just it," Aimee insisted. "They get everything they want, even if they don't deserve it. You can't let them have this. It's too important."

"I agree. And actually, somehow I've been put in charge of making sure that they *don't* have this." Maggie quickly explained what had happened at the swim team meeting earlier.

"That's great news!" Aimee uncapped the pen and checked off something in her notebook. "So I had some ideas."

"Ideas?" Maggie hoped she didn't sound as confused as she felt. It wasn't because Aimee wanted to help—Aimee was always helpful. It was because Maggie hadn't even come up with anything yet. And of the two of them, Maggie was the better planner.

"First," Aimee continued, "I think we should start a petition."

"A petition."

"Yes. I think we should get to school early and stay late, and position ourselves by the front doors so we get every single kid coming and going."

"Okay." Maggie watched Aimee write something in the paper's margin. "Petitions are good . . ."

Aimee looked up from the notebook. "But?"

Maggie paused. "But I'm just not sure who'll sign it. I mean, besides you, me, and the rest of the swim team. I don't think the board will be swayed by fifteen signatures—especially if they're all from us."

Aimee turned to the next page. "We have twenty-three non–swim team petitioners so far. I don't have their signatures yet, but I will. I've already called around and gotten verbal commitments."

Maggie tilted forward for a better view of the notebook. Aimee had written the names, numbered them, and even included the time of every phone call, apparently so she had proof of the conversations in case people tried to change their minds.

"I'll make more calls tonight to start spreading the word. Everyone thinks everyone else loves the Water Wings, but that's not really true. They're just very good at getting people to think what they want them to—including that they're more popular than they are. A lot of people know what they're really like, and after this, we'll make sure *they* know it too."

Maggie didn't say anything. She appreciated Aimee's

enthusiasm, but thought it sounded more anti–Water Wings than pro–swim team. That wasn't how Aimee usually operated.

"I also think we need money."

"To bribe the board members with cold, hard cash?" Maggie asked lightly.

"If we raise enough on our own," Aimee said, "we can convince the board that we take the swim team much more seriously than the Water Wings take their team."

"Another good idea," Maggie said tentatively, "but will that really work at this point? I mean, we've had fundraisers before, and plus, we only have a month. We'd have to sell a *lot* of cookies and brownies."

"A month is thirty days. That's a lot of time. A person's whole life can change in thirty days."

Maggie nodded. She couldn't argue that.

"Girls?" Maggie's mom knocked on the bedroom door. "The hot chocolate and granola bars are ready whenever you are!"

Maggie opened her mouth to say they'd be out in a little while, but closed it when Aimee hopped off the bed.

"The last homemade anything I had was the whole-wheat vegetable lasagna your mom made for dinner last week," Aimee said, shooting a smile over her shoulder as she hurried toward the door. "I'll get some for both of us."

Maggie waited until she heard Aimee's voice mixing with her mom's in the kitchen down the hall before crawling to the open notebook. There were at least ten pages of ideas about how to kick the Water Wings out of the pool for good. Aimee's handwriting was as messy as always— her letters sometimes tilted left, other times right, and her *O*, *G*, and *C* all looked the same—but overall, the notes were much neater than those she usually took for school. They were more organized, too, and divided into categories and subcategories. If it didn't look like they were written by a right-handed person holding the pen with her left hand, the notes could've been from one of Maggie's notebooks.

"Oh, my goodness, it's *amazing*, Mrs. Bean! You should totally have your own cooking show, or come out with a cookbook."

Maggie quickly flipped the pages back. Aimee's voice was getting louder as she headed back to Maggie's room.

"Hang on, Aimee," Maggie's mom called from the kitchen. "Take a few of these peanut-butter energy bars too. I tried a new recipe and would love your opinion."

As Aimee's footsteps receded back to the kitchen, Maggie flipped open the notebook again . . . and froze when she saw what was written on the first page.

Aimee had said a person's whole life could change in thirty days. But Maggie hadn't known that the life Aimee had been referring to was her own.

Because on the very same day that Maggie would find out whether the swim team was saved, Aimee would decide if she wanted to live with her mom or her dad once they were officially divorced.

7. Maggie sat in the middle of Arnie's bedroom floor surrounded by her laptop, stacks of colored index cards, and about a hundred pairs of socks. While she entered the Patrol This kids' names, contact information, and weights into the computer, Arnie attacked a stuffed laundry bag.

"Are you winning?" She kept typing as she looked up and smiled.

He threw one more punch, then reached in the bag and took out a clean towel. "In the brutal battle of chubby kids versus exercise, yes. I'm actually so far ahead, I don't think I can ever lose."

"Wars have been lost because of overconfidence," she warned. "You think your enemy's crying in defeat behind the bushes, sit down for a quick snack, and then, bam—sneak attack. You never saw it coming."

He turned to her and grinned. "You look cute."

She looked down as her cheeks warmed. Talk about a sneak attack.

"How's it going, anyway?" Patting his face with the towel, he stepped carefully around the socks and index cards and crouched next to her. "If you need more time, I can keep myself busy. I still have to record the workout for the Abdominator and come up with its clever name."

"How about the Knockout?" Maggie offered.

He bumped his shoulder lightly against hers. "I think that might be confusing. Unless we put your picture where mine is on the website."

"I still have a ton of information to enter." She pointed to the laptop screen so he wouldn't look at her face and see the pink in her cheeks traveling down her chin and all the way to her neck. "Unfortunately, Electra doesn't believe in typing. Or alphabetizing."

"Why bother, when you can pay someone else to do it?" Arnie asked logically.

"True," Maggie said. "So, I've divided up all the cards into boys and girls piles, and now I'm entering all their information. Eventually, once everything's in, I'll sort the list alphabetically and attach the pictures that we took at the last meeting. Then we'll know who's who and can find out how to reach them in about two seconds."

"Brilliant."

"And it's so easy to maintain," Maggie added excitedly. If Arnie were anyone else, she would've already stopped herself, but she knew he didn't mind her enthusiasm for things most everyone else their age considered dorky and boring. "I mean, we had three new kids at the meeting today, and who knows if more will show next week. But if they do, I can just enter a new line, re-sort it, and it will be like they've been with us since the beginning."

Arnie eyed the index cards lined next to the laptop, which were the next ones up for entry. "So I take it I should bust out the digital camcorder?"

She followed his gaze to the cards, and then looked at the laptop screen. She still had seventeen kids to go. She knew the project would bug her until it was finished, but at the rate of five minutes per entry, finishing would take almost an hour and a half. And according to her schedule, this was Arnie time—not Patrol This time. She'd allowed a brief overlap because Arnie had had a stroke of genius during the drive from the meeting to his house and wanted to try out his new laundry-bag-as-punching-bag exercise idea, but now that he was done, she should be too.

"Nope." She saved the spreadsheet and closed the laptop. "I'm all yours."

He grinned like she'd just told him Nike wanted to buy the rights to his kid-friendly workouts.

"What should we do?" she asked.

"Well . . ." He stood up and walked over to the closest window. "My parents are at the club all day for some charity golf tournament, and I told Little Mom and Dad Junior that they should take advantage of the absence and enjoy the afternoon. Their cars are gone, so it looks like they both took me up on it."

Maggie was so busy trying to decide if it was funny or sad that Arnie referred to his nanny and driver as his second set of parents, she didn't immediately get why he was announcing their whereabouts.

He looked at her. "Which means Casa Gunderson is all ours."

"Oh." She wished she'd left the laptop open after closing the document so she'd have something to focus on. Because now not only was her face tomato-red, she was also having a hard time blinking. "So we're all alone?"

He nodded, and his grin grew wider.

"Great." She swallowed and tried to force her lids

down over her eyes. "That's really great."

"You want something to drink?"

"I would *love* something to drink," she said, her eyes finally snapping shut as she jumped up from the floor.

She followed him out of the room and downstairs, not sure why she was suddenly so nervous. They'd been by themselves many times before, and it had never bothered her. In fact, being alone together was usually exactly the same as *not* being alone together. When they were by themselves, they still talked, laughed, and played video games, just like they did whenever parents were nearby.

But being alone felt different now. Probably because *they* were different now. They were no longer just good friends, or Pound Patrollers allies, or the Patrol This dream team. They went on dates—or, they'd gone on *one* date, anyway, and planned to go on more. She'd already started silently referring to him as her boyfriend, even though they hadn't actually discussed their official status yet.

"Water?"

"I *love* water," she said, a bit too enthusiastically. She was glad when he took a bottle from the refrigerator and handed it to her without asking why she sounded like she'd just crossed the blazing hot Sahara.

"By the way," he said, taking a bottle for himself and

leaning against the counter, "I meant to ask. Did you change your locker?"

She pressed her lips together to keep the water she'd just swallowed from shooting back out. "My locker?" she said once it had successfully made it all the way down her throat.

"Yeah. Pete said he hasn't seen you once since school started, and asked if you were okay. He thought you might've moved again, to somewhere out of the district."

"Nope," she said brightly. "Didn't move."

"Well, *I* know that. I told him I've seen you a lot since school started, and that you're totally fine. So then he thought maybe you'd changed lockers for some reason, because last year, he saw you between classes all the time."

All the time. That was probably fairly accurate, since last year, she'd made it a point to go to her locker after every class. Nothing had made her happier than the possibility of seeing and talking to Peter Applewood every forty-five minutes.

But that was last year. This year, her happiness had a very different source.

"I just don't go as much," she explained. "My classes are scattered throughout the building, so it's not always easy to make it all the way to one end to go to my locker, and then all the way to the other end for class in three minutes. And

I always end up having to take every single book home for homework anyway, so I just carry them with me during the day. That's all."

That definitely wasn't all, but there was no way she was going to tell Arnie the real reason she didn't go to her locker. She couldn't tell him that she was scared of what she and Peter would say to each other when they were by themselves (in a crowded hallway) for the first time since she'd told him she liked him. She didn't even know if Arnie knew that she'd once felt that way about Peter, let alone that she'd told him and been rejected. Arnie and Peter were cousins, and close . . . but they were still boys. She hoped that when they talked, they stuck to sports and games instead of girls. Not only was what happened between her and Peter painfully embarrassing, she also didn't want Arnie to ever think that he was runner-up, or her second choice.

He raised his eyebrows. "I've seen your backpack filled to maximum capacity. It's bigger than the Empire State Building, and probably weighs more too. You're telling me you haul that thing around for seven hours every day?"

She put the water bottle on the counter, pushed her sleeves up to her shoulders, and lifted both arms. As she flexed, she pouted just like his Abdominator picture on the Patrol This website.

He nodded. "Kind of scary that my girlfriend's biceps are three times bigger than my own, but I can respect it."

Still flexing, she looked at him.

He was about to take a sip from his water bottle, but stopped. "You're not going to put those to use right now, are you? And demonstrate their power by shattering the fruit bowl into a million pieces with just one punch?"

"Your girlfriend?" she asked, slowly lowering her arms. If she'd been able to think of anything but that one word, she might've tried to tone down the smile that was automatically lifting her cheeks. "Did you just call me your girlfriend?"

He paused, then tilted his head back and drained the water bottle in three big gulps. He kept his eyes on the ceiling for a second. When he looked at her again, his face was scrunched up, like he was nervous—scared, even. "Aren't you?"

Her head spun. If he thought she was his girlfriend, then it was okay for her to think of him as her boyfriend. Which meant that they were no longer inching along toward couple-dom—they were already there.

"I mean, I know we haven't actually been *out* that much, but in a way, it feels like we've been together forever. If I'm totally ahead of myself, then we can definitely—"

He stopped talking when she ran over to him, threw her arms around his neck, and squeezed. His whole body was tense at first, but when she didn't let go right away, he relaxed enough to put his arms around her waist and hug her back.

"This might be my new favorite exercise," he said, and she could hear the smile in his voice. "It might not burn very many calories . . . but I'd stop eating to make up for it."

"We should probably practice it a lot before recording it for the Abdominator," Maggie said into his shoulder.

They stayed like that for a minute, until the phone rang. As Arnie ran to answer it, Maggie leaned against the counter and looked around the kitchen. This was where she'd told Peter that she liked him as more than a friend. And this was where he'd told her he liked her as *only* a friend. They'd sat on the tall stools by the center island while Aimee distracted Arnie by asking about the fancy towels in one of the house's many bathrooms. Maggie'd been so upset that shortly afterward, she ate three slices of gooey, greasy pizza to try to smother the aching in her belly.

That aching had been gone a while, but now there was no chance of it returning. Eating *twelve* slices of gooey, greasy pizza wouldn't have the same effect that being Arnie's girlfriend did.

"Good news," Arnie said, coming back into the kitchen. "Little Mom and Dad Junior are partying at Target like it's Disney World, and then they're going to Applebee's for potato skins and margaritas. They won't be back for a few hours, and the other parental units won't leave until the club kicks them out and locks the gates. Which means we have *plenty* of time to do something we've never done before."

"Great," Maggie said, more sincerely than before. For some reason, the idea of being alone with Arnie seemed less intimidating now.

He smiled at her, then took her hand and led her out of the kitchen.

"Where are we going?" Maggie asked as she followed him through a series of rooms and hallways she'd never been in.

"I don't believe in keeping secrets from your loved ones," he said as they reached a shiny, closed wooden door at the very back of the house. "I mean, besides your parents. It goes without saying that that's not only okay, but necessary."

"Definitely," Maggie agreed, trying to focus on Arnie's words and his fingers wrapped around hers at the same time.

"But my dad keeps a very big secret from my mom. The only reason *I* know about it is because Little Mom and Dad Junior get loose in the lips when I put on my iPod and they think I can't hear them talking." He looked at her. "But I hear everything."

"Of course you do."

Arnie put one finger to his lips to remind her that what she was about to see was to be kept between them, and opened the door.

Maggie gasped.

"Not bad, right?" Arnie sounded pleased.

"Why would anyone want to keep *this* a secret?" She hardly felt her feet on the floor as she entered the room and walked across the thick, plush carpet.

"You've met my mother. She's small, but she can do some serious damage."

"True, but still." Maggie stood in the middle of the room and turned slowly. A floor-to-ceiling movie screen took up an entire wall. Four reclining, navy blue seats that looked like they could fit three people in each faced the screen. A glass cabinet filled with Twizzlers, Milk Duds, Sour Patch Kids, M&M's, popcorn, pretzels, and cans of soda sat against the back wall. "This is a real movie theater—in your *house*. What's not to like?"

"My mom's idea of a fun movie night is watching a documentary about the Civil War or Einstein's Theory of Relativity—the more educational, the better. My *dad*'s idea of a fun movie night is watching anything with car chases and explosions—the noisier, the better. Mom would flip if she knew Dad occasionally liked to unwind by shutting off his brain for a few hours every now and then."

"Well," Maggie said, flopping into the closest chair and smiling up at him, "thank you for letting me in on the secret."

"I know you can keep it." He squeezed her hand, and then gently let it go. "Don't move. I'll be right back."

Don't move. She probably *should* move—an action-packed blockbuster would last at least two hours, and she still had to finish the Patrol This spreadsheet, read fifty more pages of *Little Women*, do twenty math problems, study for a history test, *and* call Aimee to check in. Oh, and save the swim team, which she hadn't gotten any closer to doing since finding out it was up to her. But she wouldn't move. She couldn't. The chair was too comfortable, and Arnie had already hit play and was in the seat next to hers before she could feel even a little bit guilty. On top of which, she was Arnie's *girlfriend*. The thought made her so happy, she might never move again.

As the lights dimmed and the movie started, Maggie suddenly knew why she'd been nervous about being alone with Arnie.

She hadn't been afraid of what Arnie would want to do when they were alone as a couple for the very first time.

She'd been afraid of what he *wouldn't* want to do. What if, after everything that had happened and everything they'd been through, he never wanted to kiss her?

But she would worry about that later. Because Arnie was her boyfriend. And he was holding her hand like he might never let it go.

8. "Aim, don't you want to wait inside?" Maggie peered out from under her heavy hood.

"Nope," Aimee said, her eyes locked on the empty circular driveway before them. "They'll be here any minute."

Maggie turned carefully to avoid spilling the water pooled in the creases of her hood onto her face, and checked the teachers' parking lot. Not only were the school buses probably still miles away, but the teachers were delayed too. There were only four cars in the parking lot. "But it's pouring!" Maggie half-shouted, turning back to Aimee. "You're standing six inches from me and I can barely see you."

"Mags, we talked about this for an hour last night. This is the plan—to get them *before* they go inside, so we can take advantage of their good moods. As soon as they walk through these doors, the reality of the school day will take over, and we'll risk losing their attention—and their signatures."

"I know that *was* the plan. But that was before we knew it was going to rain cats and dogs. And goats, sheep, horses, pigs, kangaroos, and every other animal under the invisible sun."

"Do you want my jacket?"

Maggie frowned. "No, thanks." Aimee's jacket didn't even have a hood. Water streamed down her face, and her blond hair was so wet that it looked brown, but she didn't seem to notice.

Aimee shrugged and hugged the petition—which was currently protected by a plastic shopping bag—to her chest.

"Aim," Maggie tried again when the rain started falling even faster, "don't you think we might lose even more signatures if we stay out here in these conditions? The reality of the school day can't be worse than getting soaking wet."

"Actually, I think this makes our jobs easier," Aimee said brightly. "We won't have to spend as much time explaining the cause and convincing people to sign, because they'll be so anxious to get inside. The conditions couldn't be better."

Maggie doubted that logic, but didn't say anything. Aimee had been so excited to meet before school and start collecting signatures, it was hard to put up much of a fight. Maggie knew this was more about Aimee focusing all of her energy and attention on something besides her parents than it was about saving the swim team or getting back at the Water Wings . . . but Aimee was her best friend. Maggie hoped she would talk about what was bothering her eventually, and if a little distraction helped her get by until then, then standing in the rain was the least Maggie could do.

"And here comes our first signature of the day," Aimee said, unwrapping the petition as a silver SUV skidded to a stop at the bottom of the steps.

Maggie squinted to try to see through the rain. The weather had to be playing tricks on her, because the SUV looked a lot like Arnie's parents' SUV, and the boy charging up the steps looked a lot like Arnie . . . but Arnie went to a private school in the next town.

"I'm so sorry!" the boy called out as he ran.

"Sorry?" Maggie blinked and shook her head. When she realized the weather wasn't playing tricks after all, her heart fluttered against her ribs. "Why? And what're you doing here?"

Arnie stopped on the step below theirs and grinned at her from under the brim of his soaking-wet baseball hat. He reached into his backpack and pulled out something long, thin, and black. "I tried your house first, but your mom said you'd already left."

Maggie looked up when a bright blue sky with puffy white clouds suddenly appeared above her.

"I wanted to get it to you before you went outside," Arnie said. "I thought it would help make your rainy day a little brighter."

"It did." Maggie thought her smile had to be as wide as the open umbrella as she took it from him. "It does. Thank you."

"Good." He returned her smile and started backing down the steps when a car horn honked. "I have to go. But I'll call you later!"

"Mags," Aimee said as they watched him jump into the silver SUV, "I think you've got yourself a keeper."

"Excuse me?" a small voice asked before Maggie could agree.

Maggie waited until the silver SUV disappeared before turning around and looking down. She wondered where the little girl with short black hair had come from, and why she wasn't at the elementary school down the block.

"You're Maggie Bean, right? The 400-meter freestyle record holder?"

"That's me." Maggie glanced at Aimee, who was watching the little girl curiously.

"Oh, my goodness." The little girl beamed and hopped up and down. Like Aimee, she didn't seem to notice the monsoon currently hurling buckets of rain at them. "It's so, so great to meet you. I think you're *such* an amazing swimmer. I didn't miss one of your meets last year—not one. I even got my mom to drive me all the way to Marshfield for your last meet of the season, even though Marshfield is, like, an hour away and my mom hates driving five minutes to go to the grocery store."

"Wow," Maggie said, confused but flattered, "that's great. Thanks for the support. But speaking of your mom . . . does she know you're here?"

"Of course. She just dropped me off. She always drops me off. We live too close for me to take the bus, but too far for her to let me walk. I'm here half an hour before the first bell rings every day, because she likes to avoid all school traffic."

She was talking so fast, Maggie had to watch her lips to make sure she didn't miss anything.

"What grade are you in?" Maggie asked when the girl finally paused to take a breath. She had to be several inches shy of five feet tall, and was so thin, she could've easily fit three more of herself in her baggy jacket. If she hadn't said she came to their school every day, Maggie would've guessed she was in fourth grade, tops.

"Sixth grade," she said proudly, holding out one hand. "I'm Carla Cooper—aka C. C., aka your biggest fan."

Maggie glanced at Aimee again. Aimee raised her eyebrows, and Maggie could tell she was trying not to smile.

"Most people in my class couldn't wait to get to middle school so they could have their own lockers and more than one teacher every day. But *I* couldn't wait to get to middle school just so I could walk the same hallways as Maggie Bean."

Maggie was slowly shifting from flattered to concerned. "Thank you. It's nice to meet you."

"It's *great* to meet you. So, so great." She winced. "Sorry, I already said that, didn't I?"

"You did." Maggie was still slightly concerned, but couldn't help but smile. She wasn't sure why Carla was such a fan—Maggie was a record holder, but not the *only* record holder—but knew how it felt to worry about not making a good impression on someone you really wanted to impress.

"So when's your first meet? I went to the swim team website to find the schedule, but it hasn't been updated since May. And I looked for flyers in the gym, but didn't see any, and then I asked Ms. Pinkerton, and she asked me if she looked like she had time to answer such ridiculous questions."

"That's our Ms. P," Maggie said. "Don't worry. You'll get used to her."

Carla smiled.

"The reason you can't find any information on the swim team schedule is because the swim team is in danger of extinction." Aimee stood by Maggie and held out her hand for Carla to shake. "Aimee McDougall. Swim team campaign manager and Maggie's best friend."

Carla's mouth fell open as she took Aimee's hand. "Extinction? But . . . why?"

"Because a crazy, lip gloss—eating swarm of silver-suited vultures are—"

"Because of budget cuts," Maggie said, cutting off Aimee in hopes of not alarming Carla more than she already was. "Apparently running the pool is very expensive, and the school can't afford to have so many swimming-related teams."

"That's crazy," Carla blurted.

"Crazy, but true," Aimee said, clucking her tongue. "You'll learn, little Carla, that life doesn't get easier just because you get older."

Carla looked at Aimee, obviously unsure of how to respond, and then at Maggie. "What will you do?"

"I'm not sure," Maggie said honestly. "But right now, I'm

hoping I'll keep swimming. We have a month to convince the school board that we deserve to hang around."

"That's why we're here now," Aimee added. "We're collecting signatures for a petition."

"In the pouring rain?" Carla asked.

"In the pouring rain," Maggie confirmed quickly, before Aimee could get defensive.

"Good idea." Carla nodded. "Get them before they have a chance to think too long about what they're signing."

Maggie looked at Aimee. Her smile was fleeting, but it was definitely there.

"Here come your petitioners."

Maggie followed Carla's nod toward the circular driveway. The first bus was screeching to a stop, and two more followed behind.

"Okay, Mags," Aimee said, taking Maggie's elbow and leading her to the middle of the top step in front of the school's main entrance. "Remember what we talked about. 'No' is not an option."

"Right." Maggie's heart started to beat faster. She trusted Aimee, but still wasn't sure that their classmates cared enough about the swim team to sign a petition. Plus, she hated being the center of attention and was seconds away from trying to talk to the entire school.

"Twenty-eight days," Aimee reminded her gently. She squeezed Maggie's hand as the first kid stepped off the bus and started running for the front door.

"Twenty-eight days," Maggie repeated, hoping this didn't up being a waste of part of that time.

The first kid off the bus was now sprinting with his head down, and taking the steps two at a time.

"Excuse me," Maggie called out.

If he heard her, he ignored her. He cleared the landing in one giant step and was on the other side of the doors before Maggie could say anything else.

Maggie turned back toward the bus. "Hi," she tried again as two girls started dashing up the steps. They looked out from under the binders they held over their heads, but continued into the building without slowing down.

"Louder," Aimee suggested, waving the clipboard that held the petition over her head.

"Good morning!" Maggie practically shouted as a group of four boys started toward the front door. They walked slowly enough that she was able to see who they were before they bolted through the doors, and she was happy when she recognized them. They were in her grade and were usually late to every class. They might actually welcome the reason to not head right to homeroom. "Hi," she said as they got closer. "I was wondering if I could borrow your ears for a second."

She tried to stay calm when they exchanged amused looks. She'd told Aimee that asking to borrow their classmates' ears wouldn't go over well. Teachers might respond well to that kind of ancient language, but kids their age would probably think they sounded like they were from another planet—just like these guys obviously did.

"Have you heard about the pool issue?" she continued before they could say anything. "And the cutbacks?"

"Yeah," one of the guys said as they paused on the landing. "And?"

Maggie glanced at Aimee, who was already holding out the clipboard expectantly.

"Well," she said, "the school wants to cut some teams. Specifically, one girls' swim team, and one boys' swim team. For the girls, that means that either the Water Wings or the regular swim team has to go. And we've started a petition to try to save the regular swim team. It does wonders for girls' morale and self-confidence, and promotes—"

"We don't really care about teams," another guy said.

Maggie's cheeks burned instantly. "Oh."

"In fact, we think school would probably be a better place without them," a third guy added. "They're too exclusive.

They promote feelings of inadequacy in anyone who isn't on one."

"Wow." She nodded. "Okay."

"But there is *one* team we support," the fourth guy said, gently elbowing one of the others. "One team that we'd probably even be cheerleaders for, it if was allowed."

"Which one?" Aimee asked when Maggie was too rattled to.

They grinned and exchanged amused looks. The fourth guy took two notebooks and held them like pom-poms as he silently waved his arms around like a bubbly cheerleader. When they'd stopped laughing, the first guy looked at Aimee's clipboard and shook his head.

"No one's better in a pool than the Water Wings," he said.

Maggie couldn't even look at Aimee as the guys moved past them and through the front doors. She stared down at the wet toes of her sneakers sticking out from the wet cuffs of her jeans and wondered why they were wasting their time. Of *course* half the school would automatically support girls who swam to be seen instead of girls who swam for sport.

She would've probably stood like that, content to hide under the hood of her jacket until the buses were empty and everyone was inside, but then a pair of bright pink rubber galoshes appeared in front of her soggy gray sneakers. Her eyes traveled slowly up, to the tops of the boots, and over a short purple skirt, a pink plastic poncho that flared out and kept the rain falling at least a foot away from the person wearing it, and a pink dome-shaped umbrella with white stars.

"Ladies."

Maggie frowned as Anabel Richards smiled at them from underneath the umbrella. Julia Swanson stood next to her, wearing the exact same raingear. Their hair was dry, and their makeup wasn't smeared. They looked exactly as they must have before leaving their houses and stepping outside that morning.

"What do you have there?" Julia asked sweetly.

Aimee moved the clipboard behind her back, but not fast enough.

"A petition?" Anabel asked, smiling at Julia. "How . . . cute."

"*A* for effort, girls," Julia said. "But you might want to head inside. Being stuck in bed with pneumonia will be boring, no matter what—but it'll be even worse knowing there's no swim team to rejoin once you're well again."

"That's *so* considerate of you," Aimee said, her voice just as sugary as theirs. "Thanks so much for looking out for us.

In return, may I suggest using your silver swimsuits as dust rags when you no longer have a reason to wear them? I hear they're great at making dull things shine."

Julia's and Anabel's eyes narrowed, but they didn't say anything else. They simply waited for Maggie and Aimee to move apart, and then walked through them.

"Maybe this isn't such a good idea," Maggie said quietly once the front doors were closed. "I don't think we should give up, but—"

Maggie stopped talking when a shrill whistle sounded behind them. The noise stopped, then sounded three more times. When Maggie was finally able to turn toward the noise's source, she expected to find whistle-happy Ms. Pinkerton standing there. Ms. Pinkerton must've overheard their exchange with Anabel and Julia and wanted to reprimand them for stooping to such low behavioral levels.

Maggie was prepared for Ms. Pinkerton's worst. But she wasn't prepared for who was standing by the front doors instead.

"What is she doing?" Aimee asked, her voice alarmed.

Maggie shook her head. She had no idea why Carla was standing in front of the main entrance with her hands on her hips, and a red whistle in her mouth.

"Listen up, people!" Carla yelled, letting the whistle drop to her chest.

Maggie raised her eyebrows. The girl was small, but her voice was very, very big.

"I know you're wet, so I'll keep this short," she continued as dozens of kids crowded the steps. "We're in the midst of a severe injustice at our school. One group of people is fighting really hard to keep their heads above water, and another group of people is trying to push them under. I know we're not all friends, or that we even get along . . . but I also know that at some point in our lives, each and every one of us has been in that same position. So if you want to support a group of hardworking peers who have done nothing but their best, if you want to help keep their heads above water, where they belong, then you will sign Aimee McDougall's petition and help save the girls' swim team."

Pulling her head back further in her hood like a turtle in a shell, Maggie scanned the crowd. The kids didn't look happy to be blocked out of the building as the rain hammered their heads and backs, but they seemed to be listening.

"Oh, one other thing!" Carla added with a quick whistle. "No one goes inside until everyone signs."

That was met with a chorus of gasps and groans, but it

got people moving. In seconds, Maggie had closed Arnie's umbrella and was sifting through her backpack for extra pens and pencils to hand out to the kids surrounding them.

"Mags," Aimee said with a smile, releasing the clipboard so people could pass it around, "you know I love you . . . but that little girl really might be your biggest fan."

9.

Maggie would never tell him so, but the more time she spent with Arnie, the more he reminded her of chocolate. It wasn't just because he was sweet, or that each time she saw him was like being presented with a beautifully wrapped box of Valentine's Day candy. It was because being near him seemed to make all her problems disappear and her stresses melt away, just like bags of Milky Ways and Snickers used to, not long ago.

"Hi," he said with a smile as she jogged up the elementary school steps.

"Hi." Her smile, which had started almost as soon as her mother's car had pulled out of the driveway ten minutes earlier, grew wider. Arnie was leaning against a railing, waiting for her. He was wearing khaki cargo pants and a green hooded sweatshirt, and his curly hair was messy and adorable. He looked like he always did, but Maggie thought he'd never looked better.

"How's the petition going?"

It was only a short sprint from the car to the elementary school entrance, but she was so excited to see him, her heart pumped like she'd just run a mile. She stopped on the step just below his to catch her breath. "The petition?"

"The one you and Aimee have been pushing all week? In support of school pool domination?"

"Oh. Right." She laughed lightly, too distracted to be embarrassed about needing the reminder—even though she really *should* have been embarrassed, since she and Aimee had discussed next signature-securing steps on the phone not even an hour ago. "It's fine."

He waited for her to elaborate, but she didn't offer anything else. She didn't know what she would've said if she could've gotten her head to stop spinning long enough to separate her thoughts into logical responses. Standing there on the steps with him, saving the swim team didn't seem like such a big deal.

"How are *you*?" she asked instead.

He looked behind her to make sure her mom had already driven away, and then took her hand and squeezed it. "Better now."

There was at least one difference between the effects that eating chocolate and being with Arnie had on her. While her stomach always felt full and heavy after having too much chocolate, it flip-flopped and fluttered like it was filled with a thousand butterflies every time she saw Arnie.

They continued to hold hands as they entered the school and walked down the main hallway. At this point a few months ago—or even a few weeks ago—she would've been reviewing that meeting's agenda, double-checking her laptop bag to make sure she hadn't forgotten anything, and trying to mentally match each Patrol This name with a face. But now, she could barely remember her own name, let alone any of the twenty-three she was still learning.

That was probably why she thought they'd accidentally stepped into the wrong classroom when they opened the door and she didn't recognize anyone right away.

She released Arnie's hand and forced her brain to focus. She scanned the room, waiting for the names to come to her as she took in the kids' faces . . . but they weren't there. She was about to lean back and check the number over the classroom door when a torpedo of lemon yellow velour shot through the crowd.

"What are we giving away?"

"What do you mean?" Arnie asked as Electra joined them by the door.

"I *mean*—where did they come from? Why are they here? Is the corporate office giving away college scholarships?"

Snapped back to reality by Electra's urgency, Maggie counted quickly. "Thirty-one."

"Thirty-one," Electra declared, clapping her hand to her forehead. "That's eight more than last time!"

No wonder Maggie hadn't recognized the kids right away. The original members were still there, but the newest members stood closest to the door, apparently waiting for instructions.

"Let's not panic," Arnie said quietly, backing out into the hallway and waving for them to follow.

"We shouldn't panic," Maggie agreed once the door was closed behind them, "but that's a lot of kids."

"And there are only three of *us*," Electra said.

"Where *did* they come from?" Maggie turned to Electra. "They're calling you to register, right?"

"They were," Electra said, shaking her head. "But I didn't get any new calls this week. They must've found out by word-of-mouth, and just decided to drop in."

"Isn't there a cap?" Arnie asked. "Or some kind of deadline? Maybe we should thank them for coming and ask them to sign up in advance for the next session."

Maggie moved away from the door as a young mother holding the hand of a chubby little girl neared the classroom.

"I don't *want* to go," the little girl whined, her face a combination of sad and scared. "Please don't make me. I'll do anything. I'll clean my room every day, and cook dinner, and cut the grass—"

"Don't *worry*, Maddie," the mother said brightly, opening the classroom door. "You're going to have a ton of fun and make a ton of new friends. I promise."

Maggie frowned. The little girl's name was so close to her own, it made her recall how much she hadn't wanted to go to Pound Patrollers the year before. Aunt Violetta had basically dragged her there kicking and screaming . . . but it had been worth it. It had taken a while, and Maggie had resisted every step of the way, but like Maddie's mother promised, she'd had fun and made friends. *And* she'd lost weight in the process. But if her parents hadn't insisted, and if Aunt Violetta hadn't dragged her when she did, Maggie might never have gone. She couldn't imagine where she'd be now if she hadn't.

"We can't turn them away," Maggie said. "It was probably really hard for those parents to get their kids here today, and if we ask them to come again in a few months, they might be too tired by then to put up the same fight."

Electra still looked concerned, but Arnie nodded.

"She's right," he said. "We'll just have to be really organized, and do the best we can."

Electra looked at the crowd through the wide window in the classroom door, and then at Maggie and Arnie. "Are you sure you guys can handle it? You're doing a wonderful job and I know you're capable of more than most kids are at your age . . . but I don't want you to get overwhelmed."

"We'll be fine," Maggie said.

"They don't call us the Patrol This dream team for nothing," Arnie added.

Maggie managed to smile as a mother, father, and young boy rounded the hallway corner and hurried toward them. With thirty-two—*thirty-three*—kids to keep track of now, she was going to need to stay focused. Which meant that at least for one hour every week, she was going to have to do her best to ignore the effects of her new boyfriend addiction.

"I hope we're not too late," the father said breathlessly.

"You're right on time." Maggie opened the classroom door. She waited for them to go inside before turning to Arnie and Electra. "Ready?"

"The Abdominator was *born* ready," Arnie said, standing up straight and squaring his shoulders.

"I hope I have enough index cards." Electra sighed.

Maggie darted inside before Arnie could catch her eye and make her laugh. She ducked and weaved through the kids and parents, and headed for the front of the classroom. As she pulled down the projector screen and took her folders and spreadsheets from her bag, Electra welcomed the new members, and Arnie set up his laptop.

"Hey," Arnie said quietly when she dropped her pen and had no choice but to crouch near him.

Maggie froze and looked at his hand on her shirtsleeve.

"The parental units are having a party tonight, so Little Mom and Dad Junior have been instructed to keep me busy—and out of the house. We're going to hit up the mall for some food and people watching. Do you want to come?"

Yes. Yes, yes, yes, Maggie's voice sounded immediately in her head. *There's nothing I'd rather do more.*

"Maybe?" she said out loud.

"Oh." The corners of his mouth dipped. "Okay. No problem. I know it's short notice, I just thought—"

"I just have to check my schedule," she said quickly. "I think I'm supposed to watch a movie with my family, but might be able to hang out before then. I'm just not sure."

"Right." He nodded. "Got it."

She clutched her folders to her chest and watched his cheeks turn pink. Part of her wanted to throw her arms around his neck and assure him that she would go to the mall with him every single night if she could, but another part of her was scared to give in and lose even more focus. They were only five minutes into the meeting, after all, and thirty-three kids and their parents were counting on her to keep it together. If she said yes right then to hanging out, she was pretty sure hanging out would be all she would think about for the rest of the meeting. And that wasn't fair to the kids.

"Hey, guys!" Arnie clapped his hands, jumped up from the chair, and hopped onto the desk. "Welcome back to Club P.T. First off, I want to welcome all of our new members. Maggie, Electra, and I are very happy you've joined us, and we look forward to getting to know you."

As Maggie smiled and waved, she hoped no one looked too closely at her face. Arnie's cheeks had already returned to their natural olive color, which clearly meant he'd moved past their conversation. But Maggie's face still shone fuchsia. She'd given him the wrong idea. She might've even upset him—which was the very last thing she wanted to do. And now she had to wait and worry for fifty-four minutes to explain herself and make it right.

"Maggie?"

Her head snapped to the left. Arnie was looking at her and seemed to be waiting for her to say something. She followed his eyes when he shifted them toward the kids without moving the rest of his body. Her cheeks felt like she'd fallen asleep under the scorching summer sun without sunscreen as she saw all thirty-three kids, their parents, and Electra watching her curiously. She opened her mouth to respond, but having no idea what she'd missed, she had no idea what to say.

"That's our Maggie," Arnie said easily when five painfully long seconds passed. "She knows the administrative stuff is boring and feels terrible asking you to do it. But a club's a club, and we need to know a little bit about our members to make sure you have the best time possible."

"Right," Maggie agreed, finally finding her voice.

"So it's okay with you if we get the weigh-in out of the way now?" he asked her, apparently for a second time. "Electra and I will take the rest of the kids out for some P.T. Frisbee while you get what you need?"

She nodded, wanting to throw her arms around him again—this time, for saving her from even worse embarrassment.

"Great." He slid off the desk, grabbed a bag of Frisbees

from the classroom closet, and started for the door in the back of the room that led to a small courtyard.

She wasn't able to move until he was outside—and out of the sight. When she could feel her arms and legs again, she went to place the folders she still held on the desk so she could find the Patrol This member information spreadsheet.

Maggie dropped to her knees when the folders suddenly slipped from her grasp and dozens of papers flew to the floor.

She grasped for the papers frantically. She didn't want to come across as a supreme klutz, and she also didn't want anyone to see what they shouldn't. A chubby kid's weight was a very sacred thing. She'd always hated knowing her own, and before Pound Patrollers, she'd never shared it with anyone not wearing a stethoscope. Patrol This promised confidentiality, and she didn't think she could live with herself if she accidentally let that information out.

"You like him, don't you?"

Maggie's hands stopped moving when another, smaller pair started gathering the papers. She raised her eyes to see Maddie kneeling across from her and smiling.

"Is he your boyfriend?"

Maggie wondered if it was too late to seek refuge underneath the desk. Another little girl had asked her this very same question during the last Patrol This session, and answering then had been much easier. Because he hadn't been. She'd been interested in someone else, and it hadn't even occurred to her to think of Arnie that way. And maybe it should've been just as easy to answer now, because "yes" was just as easy to say as "no." But, like the members' weights, her relationship status with Arnie was confidential. Even Electra didn't know. And for Maggie's sanity—and the success of the entire Patrol This program—she wanted to keep it that way.

"Do *you* have a boyfriend?" Maggie asked instead of answering.

Maddie's face scrunched up. "*Please.* I'm nine years old. I don't have time for boys."

Maggie smiled as Maddie handed her the papers she'd gathered without looking at them, and rejoined her mother at a nearby desk.

Nine-year-old Maddie didn't have time for boys. And thirteen-year-old Maggie knew how she felt.

10.

"We're up to ninety-seven signatures," Aimee whispered, leaning across the aisle that separated her desk from Maggie's. *"Ninety-seven!"*

"I don't think I've met that many people in my entire *life*," Maggie whispered back. "And they really knew what they were signing?"

Aimee held up the clipboard. The big red letters taped to the top screamed "SAVE THE GIRLS' SWIM TEAM!" and were probably visible from the other side of the classroom.

"You wanted to make sure we were getting the message across," Aimee said. "Trust me—there's no missing this message."

"Good work, Campaign Manager," Maggie said approvingly. While ninety-seven signatures were impressive, they wouldn't have meant very much to her if her classmates had offered them simply because Aimee had asked—or demanded—them to. This way, when Maggie submitted the petition to the school board, she could feel confident that the team really had the support it suggested.

"Who kissed who?"

Maggie looked up to see which of her classmates had been caught passing notes. Ms. Pinkerton was serving as an emergency substitute for their history teacher, Miss Wells, who'd come down with acute appendicitis the night before. Most substitutes usually gave an in-class assignment to keep students busy, and then turned a blind eye and spent the next forty-two minutes e-mailing, texting, or reading magazines. Because most substitutes were smart enough to know that it was impossible to gain the respect of twenty eighth graders in a single period.

But, not surprisingly, Ms. Pinkerton was *not* most substitutes.

"Who was making out? Who broke up? Whose little romantic escapades are so important that you simply can't wait for the bell to ring to start picking them apart like hawks on roadkill?" Ms. Pinkerton leaned back in her chair and crossed her arms over her chest. "Please. Indulge me."

Maggie winced at Ms. Pinkerton's tone as she scanned

the room for the poor victims—and then slowly slid down her seat when every single one of her classmates turned and looked in her direction.

"Bean," Ms. Pinkerton barked. "McDougall. I'm sure we'd all enjoy a good love story right about now. Isn't that what history's about, after all? The events that occur as a result of people coming together, being torn apart, and leaving entire continents reeling in their wake?"

"Well," Maggie started, "sort of, but—"

"Ms. P," Aimee said sweetly, "Maggie and I weren't gossiping. Like you, we have more important things to do than worry about the dating trials and tribulations of our peers. In fact, we were just—"

Aimee stopped when Ms. Pinkerton held up one hand—which, Maggie couldn't help but notice, must've just had an at-home manicure. Ms. Pinkerton's previously nonexistent fingernails were now covered by neon pink, clawlike tips.

"Please. That's enough. I enjoyed every bite of the cheeseburger with extra cheddar, fried onion rings, and mayonnaise I had at lunch . . . but I don't need to taste it again."

Maggie and Aimee exchanged looks as Ms. Pinkerton slowly pushed her chair away from the teacher's desk and stood up.

"You're right about one thing, McDougall," Ms. Pinkerton

said, wobbling across the room in yellow sandals with three-inch heels. "You do have more important things to worry about than your classmates' out-of-control hormones."

Maggie bit her bottom lip to keep from smiling as a series of groans sounded throughout the room. Her classmates had a hard enough time staying serious when discussing anything related to the human anatomy in science class . . . but hormones and Ms. Pinkerton were definitely a bad combination.

"Now," Ms. Pinkerton continued, "I haven't talked to Miss Wells or her doctors, so I don't know how long she'll be recovering, when she'll be back at school, or if she was really even sick to begin with."

"What do you mean, you don't know if she was really even sick to begin with?" asked Luke Garzo, one of Maggie's classmates. "Principal Marshall said she was in so much pain last night, she could hardly walk."

"Maybe so." Ms. Pinkerton's heels clicked against the linoleum as she walked to the classroom closet. "But wouldn't *you* be hurting—or calling in sick and hiding out in fear and embarrassment—if you knew you were about to inflict this kind of torture on your unsuspecting students?"

Maggie watched her classmates exchange worried looks as Ms. Pinkerton threw open the closet door.

"What is *that*?" Luke asked suspiciously.

Ms. Pinkerton stepped back from the closet so that they had an unobstructed view. The closet was filled from top to bottom with textbooks, binders, folders, and thick stacks of paper held together with rubber bands.

"*That* is what I've been instructed to give you while Miss Wells lounges in her flannel pajamas and watches SOAP-net."

"But we already got our textbook for this class," Polly Crews said.

"*World History: A Complete Overview*," Ms. Pinkerton said with a nod. "The state requires every eighth grader to at least pretend to read that, so you'll need to hang on to it."

"So then what's with the miniature bookstore?" Aimee asked.

Ms. Pinkerton took a deep breath and clasped her hands behind her back. "Young, pretty, blond Miss Wells, who's been voted Teacher of the Year five years running, has decided to use her popularity to try to implement academic change."

"Academic change?" Polly repeated doubtfully.

"What kind?" Maggie asked, growing concerned.

Instead of answering, Ms. Pinkerton turned back to the

closet and removed a hardcover textbook, another paperback book, a three-ring binder, and a stack of rubber band–bound papers. As she carried them to Miss Wells's desk, her shoulders slumped forward from the weight.

Maggie jumped when Ms. Pinkerton dropped the books to the desk. The noise was like a grenade detonating.

"This is about as much information as teachers have to learn before they're certified to teach," Ms. Pinkerton said. "And it is all the information Miss Wells would like you to learn in this class."

Maggie's eyes widened as the class exploded in protest.

Ms. Pinkerton didn't respond to the outburst. She waited until the yelling dulled to grumbling before continuing. "In order to learn as much as possible in her absence, your history teacher wants you to read and memorize every word on every page in that stack, and prepare a syllabus."

"What's a syllabus?" Luke asked suspiciously.

"An outline," Ms. Pinkerton explained. "You're to take those thousands of pages and condense and organize the information so that it could be easily taught to other eighth graders."

"But . . . isn't that, like, the *teacher's* job?" Polly asked.

"Miss Wells seems to think that this new method will help you remember who chopped whose head off in various battles throughout time better than simply reading the state-required textbook, taking tests, and writing papers." Ms. Pinkerton paused. "Though you'll still have to do all those things too."

While her classmates groaned and shrieked, Maggie tried to stay calm. They didn't have all the details yet. Maybe the assignment was for extra credit, which Maggie always appreciated the chance to get but usually didn't need. And maybe it wasn't due until the end of the school year. If the assignment wasn't due for another ten months, she could probably start it in five months and still finish on time. That would make the second half of the year tough . . . but given the swim team situation, she might not have as much to do then, anyway.

Still, there was one other problem. As Ms. Pinkerton continued to unload the closet's contents onto her desk, Maggie worried her body would snap in half if she had to carry even one more book without going to her locker.

"So I hope you didn't have any big plans this weekend," Ms. Pinkerton bellowed over the noise as she pulled another stack of books and papers from the closet. "Or any weekend between now and Christmas, for that matter. The final syllabus is due at the end of the semester, and Miss Wells wants weekly summaries and reports to make sure you're staying on track. Your first report is due Monday."

"But Monday's in three days," Luke said, as if Miss Wells and Ms. Pinkerton had forgotten. "I have a baseball game on Saturday."

"I have a family reunion on Sunday," Polly added.

Maggie swallowed. In addition to her regular homework and weekly family fun time, she had a Patrol This meeting and a swim team strategy meeting with Aimee that weekend. Most important, she had a date with Arnie on Saturday night. She'd already organized her schedule, and every minute was accounted for.

"Well," Ms. Pinkerton said, dropping another load of papers and books on Miss Wells's desk, "you're young. You can sleep when you're old and alone and have nothing better to do."

Maggie snuck a glance at Aimee, who was looking at Ms. Pinkerton like she had an extra head growing underneath her Yankees baseball hat. Making students squirm usually brought Ms. Pinkerton great joy, but she sounded almost as unhappy with the assignment as Maggie and her classmates were.

"Blue sweatshirt."

Maggie looked away from Aimee to see Ms. Pinkerton nod at Luke.

"Why don't you and orange T-shirt make yourselves useful and start handing these out?"

Luke rolled his eyes at Adam Jackson. Apparently, Adam's bright orange T-shirt had made him an easy target for Ms. Pinkerton. As the girls' gym teacher, she didn't know the boys' names—though Maggie was surprised she didn't know Luke and Adam. They were two of the baseball team's best hitters. Maggie didn't usually follow any school sports besides swimming, but not long ago, she'd attended every baseball game and studied the team's yearbook picture like she was going to be asked to arrange the players by height. Because not long ago, she'd had one very important reason to pay more attention to baseball than any other school sport—including swimming.

Peter Applewood.

"You might want to save your energy, Bean. You're going to need it."

Maggie's hand froze, and she quickly lowered it. She was suddenly so distracted, it took her a second to realize she'd already raised it to get Ms. Pinkerton's attention. "I have to go."

Ms. Pinkerton looked up from the piles on the desk and cocked an eyebrow at Maggie.

"To the bathroom." She didn't have to go to the bathroom—and definitely wouldn't have announced it so publicly if she did—but besides faking fainting and being whisked away to the nurse's office, she knew it was the only thing that could get her out of class before the bell. "I have to go right now."

Ms. Pinkerton glanced at the clock over the classroom door. "Your bladder can't hold out for six more minutes?"

"No." Maggie prayed Ms. Pinkerton wouldn't ask any other questions. As it was, six minutes was pushing it. She couldn't afford any delays.

"You might want to get that checked out." Ms. Pinkerton didn't sound pleased, but she turned back to the closet without saying Maggie couldn't go.

"We'll talk at lunch," Maggie whispered quickly to Aimee as she jumped up.

Maggie's backpack was now so stuffed with books and folders, she could no longer zip it shut. She had to carry it in front of her at all times, because if she tried to give her arms a rest and wear it on her back, everything inside would immediately fall out. That was challenging *and* exhausting; her arms were fairly strong from swimming, but pushing and pulling water wasn't the same as hauling around thirty extra pounds every forty-five minutes. Maggie couldn't believe she'd carried around even more than that every minute of every day before she lost weight.

Which was why she had no choice. If she was going

to make it through the school year without collapsing, she would have to lighten her load. And since it wasn't possible to drop a class or two to get rid of a few books, there was only one way to do that.

She would have to go to her locker.

Her biceps felt like they were going to rip through her sweater sleeves by the time she reached the front of the classroom. She forced her arms up an extra inch to rest her backpack on the edge of Miss Wells's desk, grabbed one of each from the stacks on the desk, and piled the books and folders on top of her open backpack. She was glad Ms. Pinkerton was too busy handing books to Luke and Adam to notice Maggie taking her own pile. She didn't need Ms. Pinkerton to ask why she didn't think she could go to the bathroom and make it back to the classroom before the bell rang.

Supporting the backpack with both arms and digging her chin into the bundle of papers on top of the stack to keep the new additions from sliding off, Maggie moved as quickly as she could through the hallway. As she shuffled along, she tried to keep her mind off the pain by thinking of other reasons to leave class early and arrive to class late. The bathroom excuse was effective, but her teachers really would be concerned if she used it every day.

Before she could come up with an alternative, Maggie rounded a corner and shuffled to a stop.

There it was. It was still beige, and scratched in the top right corner. It still had a long, blue stain running along the bottom from an unfortunate pen accident last year. And it was still as pretty as she'd remembered.

Her locker. She'd missed it more than she realized.

Despite her reasons for being there, she couldn't help but smile as she dropped her backpack to the floor and spun the dial. Her fingers stopped turning automatically, as if they were biologically wired to turn the dial left to 36, right to 24, and left again to 36. Last year, her locker combination had been a glaring, frequent reminder that her figure was nothing like those of magazine models. Now, it reminded her how far she'd come since then. And that almost made her forget why she'd gone to such lengths to avoid her locker for so long.

"Maggie?"

Almost.

"Hey, Peter." She tried to turn around to face him, but couldn't. What was he doing here? Why wasn't he in class? Her heart slammed against her chest as she tossed as many books as her hands could hold into her locker. "How's it going? How was the rest of your summer? How are your teachers this year?"

"Well—"

"Oh, would you look at the time!" she declared, checking her wrist, even though she wasn't wearing a watch. "I have to be . . . somewhere . . . like, now. But we'll catch up soon!"

She bolted down the hallway and resisted fanning her burning face until she was around the corner. Darting into an empty classroom, she closed the door behind her and dropped into a desk chair.

She knew she was being silly. She knew she couldn't avoid Peter all year. And she knew that if she tried to carry all of her books without ever going to her locker next year, when they were in high school, her fingers would be too weak to hold a No. 2 pencil by the time the SATs rolled around two years later.

But that was next year. And she hadn't planned that far ahead.

11. "Mag Pie . . . I think we need to talk."

"Okay." Maggie nodded as she typed. When she reached the end of the sentence, she checked the time in the top-right corner of the computer screen and then continued typing. "We have four minutes. What's up?"

"Maggie."

"I'm listening, I promise. I just need to finish this one para—" Maggie stopped short when her mother's hands grabbed both of hers and squeezed.

"Sweetie, please save whatever you're working on and close the computer."

"Mom, I know four minutes doesn't sound like much time, but I can still get a lot done while we talk."

Her mother's fingers tightened around hers.

Maggie looked at her notes on the screen, and then at her mother. "What is it?" she asked, refraining from adding that whatever they had to talk about, it had better be important.

Her mother loosened her grip but continued holding Maggie's hands. Her eyes traveled from Maggie to the computer screen, and back to Maggie.

Sighing, Maggie hit the "save" icon and reluctantly lowered the laptop screen. Her mother didn't release her hands until the screen clicked shut and its red power light dimmed. When Maggie finally looked away from the computer, she was surprised to see that her mom looked serious—almost worried. "What's wrong?" she asked, feeling immediately guilty for having been too involved in her homework to notice that something was up. "Is it Dad? Is his cholesterol high again? Do we need to find lower low-fat cheese?"

Her mom tilted her head. "Your father's fine. So is Summer. So am I. So is everyone else we know and love."

Clueless as to what else could be wrong if her family was fine, Maggie sat back and braced for whatever it was her mother was about to tell her.

"Maggie . . . there's no desk in here."

Maggie shook her head slightly, not following.

"There's no desk in here . . . because we're in the car."

Her mother said this gently but firmly, as if she didn't want to tell Maggie the obvious but felt like she had to.

"Mom," Maggie said, her voice equally gentle yet firm, "are you *sure* you're okay?"

Her mom leaned toward her and tucked a stray strand of hair behind Maggie's ear. "Sweetie, I'm worried about you."

"Me?" Maggie was genuinely taken aback. "Why?"

"Because you're going on a date with Arnie—"

"But you love Arnie."

"You're right. I do. Which is why I can't help but wish that, during the drive here, you were gazing out the window and daydreaming about all the fun you're going to have tonight instead of staring at the computer screen."

"Mom, I appreciate the concern—I think—but I really don't have time for daydreaming. Would you like to see my schedule?" She went to open the laptop again, but stopped when her mom pressed down on it to keep it closed.

"Mag Pie, Arnie's a great guy. You're a great girl. And, trust me—I'm not trying to fast-forward your relationship or encourage you to put it before everything else, including your schoolwork. But I also don't want you to miss out on some of the best parts of being in a brand-new relationship."

Maggie frowned. "Like daydreaming?"

"Like daydreaming. It might not sound like much, but ignoring reality for a few minutes in anticipation of seeing someone you care about can be very, very exciting."

Maggie considered this. She couldn't be anywhere but in the moment when she was actually *with* Arnie—they had so much fun together that that was impossible—but lately, she definitely hadn't been devoting as much time to Arnie when they weren't together. She didn't doubt what her mom was saying, but she also didn't know how to turn off her brain and make time for daydreaming. Especially when she'd typed three whole pages of Civil War notes on the drive from their house to Sugar Plum Farm.

"Sugar Plum *Farm*?" Maggie asked suddenly, shifting in her seat and looking out the window. "As in an actual farm, with chickens, pigs, and dirt?"

"And fruit, vegetables, and flowers," her mother said, sounding puzzled. "Isn't this where Arnie said to meet him?"

"It is." Maggie took in the small wooden building, the fenced-in area that served as a miniature petting zoo, and the people carrying red wooden baskets filled with produce. "But I just assumed Sugar Plum Farm was a cute name for, like, a shopping center or mall or something."

Her mom didn't say anything, but Maggie knew what she

Tricia Rayburn

was thinking: that if only Maggie had looked up from her computer screen long enough to think about it, she might've had fun coming to a different conclusion.

"There he is," Maggie said, smiling automatically as soon as the Gundersons' silver SUV pulled into the dirt parking lot. She turned back to her mom. "Thank you for the advice. I promise I won't think of school, homework, or anything or anyone else but Arnie for the next few hours." More specifically, she wouldn't think about anything or anyone but Arnie until nine o'clock, which was when he would drop her off at home and she'd start the next chapter of her history reading. But she kept that part to herself.

She gave her mom a quick hug, grabbed her purse from the floor, and hopped out of the car. The distance between her, school, the swim team, and all of her other responsibilities grew as she hurried across the parking lot. If anyone had asked what she'd learned about the northern and southern states in the post–Civil War era just before getting in the car to drive to Sugar Plum Farm, she wouldn't have been able to answer. Because for better or worse, by the time she reached Arnie, there was just Arnie.

"Hi," she said, aware of her heart rate picking up speed.

"Hi, yourself." His lips twitched like he was trying not to smile as he climbed out of the car. "Your purse, please."

"My purse?" She looked at Arnie's outstretched hand. "What for? Lips chapped? Hands dry? Run out of your favorite vanilla-scented lotion?"

"Hey." He glanced around to make sure no one was listening. When he spoke again, his voice was softer. "We discussed that. No one but you and me needs to know about my appreciation for girly pampering products."

She tried to keep her face as serious as his. "I'm happy to share my lotion, but we might have to come up with some kind of weekly allowance. A dollop a day will have to suffice, and you'll have to learn to use it sparingly."

"You don't know what we're doing tonight—and potentially for the rest of our lives. You might want to reconsider those terms."

She pretended to think about it. "Nope."

The right corner of his mouth twitched, and then the left, until his face finally cracked in a big, crooked grin. "I had a whole thing planned, you know."

"Thing?" She smiled as he took her hand in one hand and waved to Dad Junior in the SUV with the other. "What kind of thing?"

"About survival of the fittest, and living off the land, and the nutritional value of snow." He squeezed her hand as they started walking toward the farm's entrance. "I was going to demand to search your purse—politely, of course—to make sure you didn't have a compass, map, or anything else that would give you an unfair advantage."

"An unfair advantage for what?"

They stopped walking, and he looked up without answering.

"'The Sugar Plum Farm Locally Grown, Regionally Famous Corn Maze'?" Maggie read aloud from the wooden sign hanging from the arm of a very tall scarecrow. "'Enter to play, prepare to stay'?"

"You haven't done it before, have you?"

"No," she said, eyeing the narrow trail before them that ran between two seemingly endless fields of towering corn stalks. "I can't say I've ever done anything with corn besides eat it."

"Oh, man," he said, groaning lightly as he patted his stomach. "You'll never have corn sweeter than the corn grown on Sugar Plum Farm. Assuming you make it out, I mean."

She looked at him. "We're actually going in there?"

"No."

Maggie breathed a small sigh of relief. She didn't go for walks or drives without knowing exactly where she was going, and she definitely didn't go for walks or drives without being able to see 365 degrees around her at all times. The corn stalks were twice her height and stood so close together, it was like looking at a solid green wall. She knew that after the maze's first turn there'd be nothing to see but leaves, kernels, and silk.

"*You're* going in there."

Maggie inhaled sharply.

"I'm going in *there*."

She followed his pointer finger toward another maze entrance on the other side of the petting zoo.

"Two entrances, one exit," Arnie said.

She looked at him. "You want to *race?*"

"I only know one person who likes to win more than me, and that's you. I thought a little friendly competition might be fun."

"What about the dream team?" she asked, hoping her voice sounding teasing and not terrified. "The dynamic duo? Aren't we better together than not?"

"Of course we are." He squeezed her hand. "And we'll be together again in no time—with one of us having a slight edge over the other."

"What about the nutritional value of snow? Why were you going to talk about the nutritional value of snow before if we're both going to be out in no time? It's not going to be cold enough for snow for at least two more months."

"I was kidding." His grin grew as he shrugged. "Everyone knows snow has no nutritional value."

She watched him, mouth open, as he started jogging backward. She didn't want to tell him the idea of running through Mother Nature's labyrinth made her nervous, and even more than that, she didn't want him to think that she didn't like his idea for their date. So she didn't say anything as he moved away from her, and eventually remembered to close her mouth.

"Have fun! I'll see you on the other side!"

She tried to smile as he blew her an exaggerated kiss— even though she thought it was tragic that she was going to die in a corn maze before she got to experience the real thing. When he reached the other entrance he faced her, raised one hand in the air, and then slowly curled his fingers, one by one, into a fist. As soon as his pinky was down, he pumped his fist and darted into the maze like the Sugar Plum Farm scarecrow was chasing him with a pitchfork.

Maggie sighed and turned back to her entrance. Arnie was right—she liked to win. She liked to be the best at whatever she attempted. But . . . racing through a maze of corn? That was for farmers, and coyotes, and little kids who grew up without television and had too much time on their hands. She'd never cheated at anything in her life, but she was tempted to now. She could ruffle her hair, sprinkle some dirt on her clothes, and wait for Arnie outside the maze exit. He would never have to know that she hadn't set foot on the trail.

But then she pictured his smile. And she knew she had no choice.

"If I'm not out before the sun goes down, please send a search party," she said to the scarecrow standing next to her.

As she stepped onto the trail she told herself that the maze was just another test. She'd taken dozens at school over the years, and had aced them all. Just because she hadn't studied for this one didn't mean she couldn't pass with flying colors. Plus, her reward at the end would be even better than an A plus with a shiny gold star. As soon as she finished, she would get to see Arnie.

Or, maybe not *quite* that soon. He might've had a thirty-second lead, but she could still beat him.

She smiled and quickened her pace as her competitive spirit kicked in. Soon she was jogging down the path, dodging parents and little kids and tuning out their voices as they discussed navigation strategies. She stayed focused and didn't think of anything but which way to turn. Every now and then she looked up to the sky; since it was late in the afternoon and the sun was already starting to set in the west, she used the lingering light to figure out which direction she was heading. When she hit a wall of corn stalks, she spun right around and tried another route. When she accidentally retraced her steps backward instead of moving forward, she quickly shook off her frustration and started jogging to make up for lost time. Her confidence was fueled by years of straight A's and gold stars, and she couldn't wait to meet Arnie at the exit and tell him he'd been right—that a little friendly competition was definitely a fun way to spend an afternoon.

She felt good. Excited. So good and excited, in fact, that she didn't notice when the sun's lingering light began to dim. She didn't notice when the voices around her grew quieter, and the trails became less crowded. She might not have noticed how late it was getting until it was so dark, she couldn't see the path beneath her feet . . . but then her right foot landed the wrong way on a stray cob of corn.

Her right leg shot out in front of her and her left leg crumpled under her as she landed hard in the dirt. "Oh, no," she whispered.

She sat up slowly and climbed to her knees. Her legs felt shaky but okay, but her right ankle throbbed like the Sugar

Plum Farm scarecrow had pierced it repeatedly with his rusty pitchfork. Afraid to try standing on it, since she was afraid she wouldn't be able to walk and make it out of the maze, she looked around her. Finally realizing the sky had gone from blue to gray, and that she was the only person on the path, she checked her watch. "Oh, no," she said again, not bothering to whisper.

It was six o'clock. She'd met Arnie at five. She'd been wandering through a field of corn for almost an hour, and had less than an hour to find her way out before the sky went completely black.

There were many things about being lost in the field that should've alarmed her immediately. Like the fact that she might be spending the night under a blanket of corn silk. And that her ankle was probably broken. And that Arnie and her family would be worrying about her, and she had no way of contacting them.

But instead, the only thing she could think about was that this little adventure was costing her a *lot* of valuable time.

Afraid to test her ankle but unwilling to lose another second, Maggie stood carefully on her good foot. She tried keeping her injured foot lifted behind her as she hopped forward, but the path was uneven and she struggled to keep her balance. After three attempts—the third of which almost sent her crashing to the ground again—she closed her eyes, took a deep breath, and slowly lowered her injured foot.

"Maggie?"

Her eyes snapped open.

"Is that you?"

She looked around, her heart racing like she was on the final lap of a mile run. It sped up even more when there was no one there.

"Great," she muttered. "It's only been an hour and I'm already hallucinating."

"Maggie, it's me. Arnie. You probably can't see me, but I can see you."

She looked around again. This time her eyes searched the corn stalks instead of the path running between them. If Sugar Plum Farm had installed hidden security cameras to prevent corn thievery and lost visitors, she'd definitely underestimated its modern advancement.

"I don't want to rush you, but it's getting pretty late . . ."

Maggie's eyes traveled up. Arnie's voice wasn't coming from inside the field of corn; it was coming from some-where above her. "Where *are* you?" she called out.

"Not far. I can tell you exactly how to get to me, if you want."

If you want. Maggie didn't know how he knew where

she was, but she was pretty sure he was hesitant to give her directions because he thought she'd want to finish what she started all on her own. And under normal circumstances, he would've been right. But these weren't normal circumstances. She was injured. And precious seconds that could've been spent reading and studying were ticking by, lost forever.

"Fine," she relented. "Go ahead. But it might take me a while, since I've been attacked by an evil ear of corn."

"What do you mean?" Arnie asked quickly, his voice tense. "Are you okay? Do you need help?"

Maggie opened her mouth to say that no, she definitely wasn't okay, that she hadn't been further from okay in months . . . but then realized she was no longer teetering on one foot. She'd been so surprised to hear Arnie calling down to her that she didn't notice when her injured foot landed on the ground—especially since her injured foot didn't seem to be all that injured.

"No," she said, taking two small steps forward. Her ankle felt tight, like it had a light weight wrapped around it, but it didn't hurt. "I think I'll make it."

"Great," he said, relieved. "So just go back about ten feet, hang a left and then a quick right, and you'll find me."

That was it? She was that close to the exit? As she followed Arnie's directions she thought she should feel happier about having come so close to finding her way out all by herself. But she wasn't happy. If anything, she was slightly annoyed. She didn't *want* to be annoyed, and definitely not at Arnie, but not only had she wasted time and almost ended up having to be whisked away by ambulance, she'd given up. She'd never skipped a single question on any test, and always finished minutes before her classmates. But she couldn't finish this test. She might as well glue three ears of corn on her chest in the shape of an F.

"Arnie?" she called out when his directions ended at a wooden ladder. "I don't see the exit."

"Can you climb? Or did the evil ear of corn tie your hands together with husks and silk before fleeing the scene of the crime?"

Maggie frowned. He was joking, but she wasn't in the mood.

"I think the county health department might want to pay a visit to Sugar Plum Farm," Maggie said, her hands and feet moving quickly up the ladder's rungs. "I'm sure they'd *love* to know the dangerous conditions visitors are expected to endure without any kind of warning or—"

She stopped when she reached the top of the ladder.

"Surprise," Arnie said quietly—almost apologetically.

Maggie looked around. They were on some kind of long

wooden platform that stood several feet above the tallest corn stalks. They were so high up, she could see dozens of paths zigzagging through the green maze, the parking lot, and even the farm on the other side of the street.

"It's in case you get lost, or need a hint," Arnie explained.

"Or want to refuel and unwind by candlelight?" Maggie asked, her voice as apologetic as his.

Because while she'd been quietly fuming about the precious time she was losing, Arnie had been arranging a romantic picnic for two. A small, round table sat in the center of the platform, covered in a blue-and-white-checked tablecloth and holding a vase of yellow sunflowers. A basket of Sugar Plum Farm grilled chicken, corn on the cob, and caramel apples sat at the base of the table. And ten tealight candles lined the platform's railings, casting a warm, fuzzy glow.

"I'm sorry if the race was a really bad idea," he said. "I just—"

"Don't be sorry." She stepped toward him, took his hand, and smiled. "It's perfect."

It really was. And she'd never deserved an F more.

12.

"Head's up," Aimee said, flopping into a folding chair. "Mini Mags, ten o'clock."

Maggie looked up from her history textbook to see Carla heading for them like an arrow from a bow.

"Have you two been shopping together?" Aimee asked. "Or discussing your outfits every night before bed?"

Maggie eyed Carla's long-sleeved T-shirt. It wasn't quite blue, and it wasn't quite purple . . . which was exactly what Maggie loved about the long-sleeved T-shirt *she* was wearing.

"Seriously," Aimee whispered as Carla neared, "today it's the shirt. Yesterday it was the corduroy skirt. The day before that, it was the patent leather belt. How does she do it?"

"I have no idea," Maggie said. "But I must admit—she looks pretty cute."

"Girls!" Carla flew at them so fast, she had a hard time stopping. She bumped into the table they sat behind and sent their water bottles rolling to the floor. "I'm so glad you're here."

"We're always here," Aimee said, retrieving the water bottles. "We sit here with the petition before homeroom, before and after lunch, and after the last bell. You know this, because you always just happen to be here at those same exact times too."

Maggie smiled. Carla had become a well-dressed shadow over the last few days, popping up wherever Aimee and Maggie happened to be collecting petition signatures or meeting about next steps for the swim team, but Maggie didn't mind. Carla didn't get in the way; most of the time she just hung back, watched, and listened. Maggie still didn't know *why* Carla was so interested in Maggie's swim team accomplishments, but she couldn't help but be flattered.

"I know you're here before homeroom," Carla said breathlessly, "but this is ten minutes earlier than you usually get here. And I wanted to catch you in time."

"In time for what?" Aimee shot Maggie a wary look.

They turned toward the front doors when something that resembled a cross between a foghorn and a cow sounded outside. The noise seemed to come from an old green pickup truck that was sagging on one side and missing the back window.

"Sorry." Carla ran for the doors as the horn sounded again. "That's my mom. I'll be right back!"

"Wow," Aimee said when Carla ran to the rear of the truck, put both hands on the cab door, and pushed.

"She's stronger than she looks," Maggie added as the truck inched forward.

Aimee turned to her. "Now that we have five seconds to ourselves, let's finish our conversation from last night. You said there was something you wanted to ask me?"

"Oh," Maggie said, her cheeks warming at the unexpected change of topic. "Right. There was."

"Sorry again for getting off the phone so fast. But Dad started yelling about a credit card and Mom started yelling about a car payment, and they were so loud, I could barely hear you."

"No problem." Maggie glanced toward the front door. Carla was still helping her mom, but she moved so quickly, Maggie didn't want to start talking about what she and Aimee hadn't gotten the chance to talk about on the night before. Maggie had wanted to ask about Aimee's parents, and since that conversation might take a while, she didn't want them to be interrupted.

"So what was it?" Aimee wiggled her eyebrows. "Relationship advice? My thoughts on whether you should make the first move on Señor Lipless?"

"Arnie has lips," Maggie said, happy to go along with Aimee's guess instead of quickly coming up with something to ask about besides her parents.

"You would never know it, considering he never uses them."

"That's not true. He used them on our last date, when he ate corn on the cob and a caramel apple. Try doing *that* without your lips."

Aimee looked at her. "*Anyway*, if you want to know my opinion, then yes. I think you should make the first move. You might send greeting cards instead of text messages, but you, Maggie Bean, are still a modern woman. If you want to kiss your boyfriend, kiss your boyfriend."

Maggie grabbed her water bottle to keep from fanning her face. Aimee was too polite to point it out, but Maggie knew her face was now a lovely shade of scarlet. And, like Aimee's parents, the reason why her skin was now on fire was too big a conversation to have right then. She'd told Aimee all about her time in the corn maze—including that it was another date that had ended without a kiss—but left out one key part. And that was that she couldn't blame Arnie for not kissing her, especially since she'd felt so bad for being annoyed that she hadn't talked much during the rest of the night. She hadn't wanted to say anything that might suggest she'd been less than thrilled with even one minute of their date, so hadn't said much at all. What should've been a romantic, sunset picnic high above the corn stalks had turned into a quiet, sticky snack time.

She wouldn't have wanted to kiss her either.

"I wanted to ask about Peter," Maggie said suddenly.

"Peter?" Aimee shook her head, like she was hearing things. "Peter Applewood?"

Maggie nodded. It wasn't true, but it *could've* been something she would've wanted to talk about with Aimee. And it was definitely better than delving any deeper into her romantic imperfections.

"Don't tell me you're actually considering going to your locker," Aimee said, reaching into her backpack for the petition clipboard. "We're only three weeks into the school year. You can still put off the inevitable for months."

"I *won't* tell you I'm considering going to my locker . . . because I've already gone."

Aimee's hand froze in her backpack. "What? When?"

"Last week." Maggie shrugged. "It was no big deal."

"That's so not true. If it wasn't a big deal you wouldn't

have waited so long to bring it up." She yanked out the clipboard and leaned toward Maggie. "What happened? Was it weird? What'd he say?"

"It *was* weird," Maggie admitted, "but I didn't actually talk to him."

"Oh." Aimee sat back, placed the clipboard on the table, and lined up a row of pens next to it. "So then why was it weird?"

Maggie was relieved when the front door flew open and Carla came flying through. "Your mom's car okay?"

"What?" Carla asked, like she hadn't just been pushing the old green truck through the parking lot. "Oh, right. It's fine. It just needs a little nudge every now and then. I'll go back out in a few just to make sure it's still moving down the street."

"Carla," Aimee said sweetly. "Why did you want to find us here earlier than usual?"

Maggie bit back a smile. Aimee sounded perfectly nice, but Maggie knew she was trying to keep Carla focused so that they could find out what she wanted, say good-bye, and get back to their conversation.

"Something happened last night." Carla pushed up her bangs with both hands, inhaled deeply, and exhaled loudly. "Something terrible. Something awful. Something that I never would've thought was possible if I hadn't seen it happen with my own two eyes."

Maggie looked at Aimee, who was watching Carla expectantly.

"And?" Aimee prompted when Carla paused for dramatic emphasis. "What terrible, awful, almost impossible thing did you see?"

"I don't like to be the bearer of bad news," Carla said. "The messenger. The person who has to tell people things they don't want to hear. The—"

"Carla," Maggie said gently, before Aimee's patience ran out. "What is it?"

Carla's eyes were wide as she looked at Maggie. "It's Anabel. And Julia. They're—"

"Here."

Maggie jumped as the heavy front doors flew open.

"You can put it all . . . right . . . here." Anabel strode across the entryway and pointed to a patch of floor directly across from Maggie and Aimee's table.

"I'm too late," Carla groaned, smacking one hand to her forehead. "I'm sorry. I should've gotten here earlier. I should've tried to find your phone number last night and called you as soon as I knew. I should've—"

"Carla." The artificial sweetness was gone from Aimee's

voice. She was ready to listen to whatever Carla had come to tell them. "What happened last night?"

Carla's face went from worried to panicked as two guys from the school football team placed a tall stainless-steel table and four matching chairs in the spot Anabel had pointed to. Once the furniture was in place, the guys, who were apparently Anabel's and Julia's new boyfriends, planted quick pecks on the girls' cheeks and jogged back outside for another load.

"It started out like any other night," Carla whispered, turning back to Maggie and Aimee. "Mom was bidding on antique cookie jars on eBay, I was reading my new *Betty and Veronica Double Digest* comic book, and Polly, our hairless cat, was sleeping under the Christmas tree."

"Your hairless cat?" Aimee asked.

"The Christmas tree?" Maggie added. "It's only September."

"Polly was a rescue and Mom likes to keep the tree up all year long," Carla explained quickly. "It's her favorite work of art."

Maggie felt Aimee trying to catch her eye, but stayed focused on Carla. Julia had joined Anabel in the entryway, and they were stringing white lights along the tall table as the boys brought in cardboard boxes and plastic bags.

Maggie didn't know what they were up to, and she wanted to get as much information as possible so she and Aimee weren't totally blindsided. "So your mom's bidding, you're reading, and Polly's sleeping," Maggie said. "What happened next?"

"The doorbell rang." Carla shook her head slowly, like she was still struggling to make sense of it all. "And it wasn't Tuesday, when Mom's Tupperware friends come over, and it wasn't Thursday, when her candle-making crew gets together. It was Wednesday. No one ever comes over on Wednesday."

"Wow," Julia called out suddenly. "Who knew tossing a little old football could make someone so *strong*?"

"Talk about tossing," Aimee muttered as one of the guys lifted an enormous box with one hand and grinned. "I think I might lose my breakfast."

"Carla." Maggie made herself look away from whatever was happening across the room. "Who was at the door? Was it Julia and Anabel?"

"Worse." Carla winced, the pain caused by the evening's traumatic events still fresh.

"What could possibly be worse than finding Brainless Barbie and Babbling Barbie standing on your doorstep?" Aimee asked.

Carla opened her mouth to answer just as the front doors swung open again. Two women wearing matching gray cashmere loungewear floated into the entryway, as if carried by the dozens of silver balloons that bobbed gently over their heads.

"No, no, *no*, girls," one of the women said, clicking her tongue against the roof of her mouth. "Have we been leaning a little too close to our open nail-polish bottles again?"

"That's not even *close* to what we discussed," the second woman said, her long blond ponytail flicking back and forth as she shook her head disapprovingly. "I told you having bananas with your cereal this morning would put you in a sugar coma."

As Anabel and Julia started pulling off the string of lights they'd just draped across the table, Carla looked at Aimee. "You asked what's worse than finding Brainless Barbie and Babbling Barbie on your doorstep?"

"Finding their mothers," Maggie said flatly. It had been almost a year since she'd seen them at Water Wings tryouts, but she recognized Mrs. Swanson and Mrs. Richards immediately.

"Why were Anabel's and Julia's mothers at your house?" Aimee whispered. "What did they want?"

Carla reached into the back pocket of her jeans, pulled out a small card, and handed it to Aimee.

"'Get in the Groove,'" Aimee read aloud. "'Let the Water Wings help you shake what your momma gave you.'"

"I guess I'm not the only one who still buys greeting cards," Maggie said when Aimee handed her the card. The front was white and featured a pair of shiny silver angel wings surrounded by small silver music notes. "I would've thought the Water Wings were more technologically advanced."

"They are," Carla said. "The e-mail reminders went out early this morning. But they had to have something to hold the bribe."

"iTunes?" Maggie's chin fell to her neck as she opened the greeting card and found the gift card inside.

"Fifteen free songs, courtesy of the Water Wings and their mothers," Carla said.

"With the promise of another fifteen when you sign their *petition*?" Aimee's voice grew louder as she leaned toward Maggie and read the inside of the card. "You've got to be kidding me."

"I wish I was," Carla groaned. "Apparently, they've been driving around and dropping off cards all week. Monday was the eighth graders, Tuesday was the seventh graders, and last night was the sixth graders."

"I was home on Monday night," Maggie said. "I didn't get a card."

"You're the competition, Mags." Aimee's eyes narrowed as she watched Mrs. Richards attach a bunch of silver balloons to one end of the stainless-steel table. "If you want to shake what your momma gave you, it's not going to be on their dime."

"But I don't understand." Maggie frowned. "It *is* a competition. They can get a thousand signatures like that, but it won't be because everyone who signs really thinks the Water Wings should stay."

"Not to mention that the petition was *our* idea," Aimee said. "They stole that, they're going to steal signatures, and they're going to try to steal the pool. They probably even stole the iTunes gift cards."

"Well, you know what they say," Carla said with a heavy sigh.

"You can take a horse to water, but you can't make him drink?" Maggie asked hopefully.

Aimee looked at her. "Who says that?"

"My mom," Maggie said. "She used to say it when Summer and I wouldn't eat vegetables. Now she says it when she gives Dad directions to whatever electronic device he can't make work."

"My mom says it too," Carla added, "except she means it literally. Our miniature pony will only drink milk."

Maggie bit back a smile as Aimee raised her eyebrows.

"But that's not what I was going to say," Carla continued, sinking into the metal folding chair next to Maggie's. "What I was going to say is that what *they* say . . . is that all's fair in love and war."

Maggie looked across the room. Carla was young, but she was right. If Anabel and Julia had enlisted their mothers and resorted to bribery to try to win the pool, then Maggie and the swim team would just have to come up with an even tougher strategy. They weren't going to lose the war without a fight.

And as for all being fair in love . . . that was true too. If a relationship was going to move forward, *someone* had to make the first move.

Who said it had to be the boy?

13. Maggie arrived at the next Patrol This meeting prepared for battle. She'd woken up extra early and jogged around the neighborhood to clear her head and get her heart pumping. After taking a shower, she'd spent an entire hour—three times longer than usual—picking out the perfect outfit, drying her hair, and putting on makeup. Before leaving her house, she'd checked her purse three times to make sure the peppermint Life Savers and mint chocolate chip–flavored lip gloss were still tucked in the small interior pocket. She and Arnie were supposed to hang out after the meeting, and she was armed and ready to make her move.

"Hi." She smiled brightly as she jogged up the elementary school steps.

"Hi." Arnie hopped off the railing he'd been sitting on and slid his hands in his pants pockets.

Maggie's heart skipped a beat when his smile seemed smaller than usual, but she quickly reminded herself that the last time they saw each other was on the corn maze date—the last part of which they'd spent picking caramel out of their teeth instead of talking. Because she'd been so quiet then, he probably wasn't sure what to expect now.

But *she* knew what he could expect. And the thought made her smile grow.

"Are you ready for another session of your adoring fan club?" She stopped on the step below his.

"My fan club?" He sounded confused. "What fan club?"

Feeling the corners of her mouth start to dip, she forced them back up. "You know the only reason these kids come here every week is to hang out with their favorite idol, mentor, and comedian. Electra and I are just there to fill in if ever you need a break. We might as well change the name from Patrol This to Abdominate This."

"Oh." He looked down at his sneakers. "I don't know about that."

Maggie kept smiling, but wasn't sure what to say as she looked down at her own feet. She couldn't see them now because they were hidden under her black ballet flats, but she'd painted her toenails pink just for their date today. She wasn't likely to take her shoes off, so Arnie probably wouldn't see them, but she just liked knowing that her toenails were polished. She felt prettier, somehow. But as they stood there not speaking, she began to doubt that that was worth the ten minutes of extra preparation.

"Maggie and Arnie, playing with the Wii . . ."

Maggie spun around. Her smile disappeared as Lenny, the Christmas vacation boy from their first meeting a few weeks ago, bounded up the steps ahead of his mother.

"K-i-s-s-i-n-g!" Lenny sang triumphantly.

"Lenny!" his mother called after him. "Go directly inside. Do not pass GO, do not collect two hundred dollars. Do you hear me?"

Maggie was relieved when Lenny didn't slow down as he puckered up and blew kisses at them.

"I'm very sorry," his mother said, hurrying after him. "Just ignore him. That's what we do."

Arnie waited until they were both inside before turning back to Maggie.

"Maggie and Arnie, playing with the Wii?" she asked.

"Apparently, the 'tree' has become the Wii," he explained. "Though as a video game expert, I have to say that I don't think it's logistically possible to kiss and hold the controller at the same time."

"Kids," Maggie said, shaking her head.

That got a small chuckle out of him, but after a few seconds they were both staring at their feet again.

"So we should probably head in," Arnie said finally.

"Good idea," Maggie agreed, following him as he turned and started up the steps. As they walked, she felt her confidence chipping away like the red polish that had been on her toenails before she'd repainted them. "Are we still hanging out today? After the meeting, I mean?"

He looked at her over his shoulder. "Sure. If you still want to."

If she still wanted to? Why wouldn't she want to? Did that mean that *he* didn't want to?

"Of course I do," she said. "Do *you?*"

"I do. If you do."

She'd already said she did, and she wasn't sure why he didn't just *know* that she wanted to hang out with him. She realized she hadn't acted quite like herself during the corn maze picnic, but that was one awkward night out of countless other amazing nights they'd hung out together. Did one less-than-perfect date discount all the perfect times that had preceded it?

Thankfully, they reached the crowded classroom before her confusion could spiral into panic. They both smiled as they stepped through the classroom door, and greeted the kids and parents like everything was fine—which Maggie really, really hoped it was.

She tried to not worry about it for the next hour. As they sat in a circle and discussed the benefits of snacking, played badminton in the courtyard outside, and weighed the kids behind the purple Patrol This curtain, Maggie focused on the meeting instead of on what had happened on the steps *before* the meeting and about what might happen *after* the meeting. And she made sure she didn't let her mind wander to the one thought that was making focusing difficult: that it would be tough to win the love battle if she was the only one participating.

"Another successful session," she said after the meeting, when the last kid-and-parent pair had left the classroom with Electra.

"Yeah." He flashed her a quick smile as he turned off his laptop and wrapped up its power cord. "Not bad."

She watched him wind the cord around his hand, and then grabbed a folder from her stack of Patrol This materials, opened it, and pretended to review some notes. Every now and then she peeked over the top of the folder, hoping— and failing—to catch Arnie looking at her. When his laptop bag was zipped and hanging over his shoulder, he scanned the room, as if searching for something else to keep him busy.

"Arnie—"

"Maggie—"

They both looked away and smiled.

"Is it me . . . ," he started after a minute, "or does this feel a little strange?"

She shook her head, simultaneously nervous and relieved. "It's not you."

"But we're . . . this . . . it's never strange."

She started to step toward him, but then remembered why they were having the conversation and stopped. "I know."

"I don't *want* it to be strange."

"Me neither," she said quickly.

He nodded. She racked her brain for the right thing to say, but had no idea what that was. Up until very recently, words had always come easy around Arnie. They were so comfortable with each other, she never had to think about what to say next, or if she said something she shouldn't, or if he meant something other than exactly what he said. This strained silence was new to them, and Maggie didn't understand it. As a couple, she thought they should be better together than ever.

"How do you feel about a do-over?" he asked suddenly.

"A do-over?"

He grinned and started across the classroom, waving for her to follow. She grabbed her folders and purse and hurried after him, turning off the light and closing the door on her way out. He stayed a few feet ahead of her as they headed down the hallway and out of the building, and didn't stop until they were back on the school steps.

Realizing what he was doing and happy for the chance to try again, Maggie jogged down the steps until she reached the step just below his. Her heart fluttered in her chest as she faced him. "Hi," she said brightly, as if this were their first encounter of the day.

"Hi, yourself," he said with a grin.

Maggie's smile was so wide, she was sure she could fit quarters in her deepened dimples. Unlike their first meeting an hour ago, Arnie looked excited instead of uncertain.

"So, I couldn't *wait* to see you today."

"Really?" she asked, her dimples now ready for silver dollars.

"Really." He held out one hand, which she took. "Those caramel apples might've tasted like heaven on a stick, but they were definitely made by the devil. I didn't check the calories beforehand because I didn't want to ruin the mood, but I had to do some serious sweating after our date. You, being the lovely, delicate lady that you are, only had one caramel apple. But I, being me, had *four* caramel apples."

"And this made you want to see me today because . . . ?"

He patted his stomach. "The Abdominator's got a new move. You have to see it. It's one part Martha Stewart, one part Kanye West, and two parts David Blaine."

"David Blaine?" Maggie asked, already laughing. "The street magician?"

"Hanging upside down like a bat doesn't burn many calories, but hanging upside down while vacuuming to some crazy hip-hop beats can really—"

"Mags!"

Picturing Arnie's latest exercise made Maggie laugh so hard, it took a second to realize someone was shouting her name up the steps.

"Maggie!"

"Is that Aimee?" Arnie asked, peering over the top of Maggie's head. "Has she been indulging in Sugar Plum Farm's famous caramel apples too? Does she need the structure and support of Patrol This to help her shed those pesky pounds?"

"She's not here for the meeting." Still giggling, Maggie wiped the tears from her eyes and turned toward the parking lot. "She's taking us to Bananarama."

"Were your parents busy?" Arnie asked, his voice slightly

concerned. "I could've asked Little Mom or Dad Junior to take us. Driving me around is kind of why my parents pay them more money than they have free time to spend."

Maggie waved to Aimee, who was leaning out of the open passenger-side window of her mother's car like she was gasping for oxygen, and then turned back to Arnie. "Remember how I said I wanted to plan today's date?"

"Yes . . . ?"

"Well, it has two parts. The *second* part is a moonlit boat ride around Mud Puddle Lake. Just us." That was when, if all went according to plan, she would engage in Operation First Kiss. "And the first part is lively conversation and fresh fruit smoothies at Bananarama . . . with Aimee."

"Oh," he said as his eyebrows lowered in confusion. "Okay."

"The first part won't take long," she promised, her lingering smile fading. "It's just that things with the Water Wings got a little out of hand this week, and Aimee really wanted to talk strategy, and since I'm technically in charge of saving the swim team, I couldn't really say no. Plus, she's kind of going through a hard time at home, and—"

"Maggie, it's fine," Arnie said.

She tried to get his eyes to meet hers. "Are you sure?" she asked. She'd been so focused on the second part of the date that she hadn't really thought much about meeting Aimee for the first. She and Arnie were friends too, so Maggie didn't think he'd mind hanging out with her for a little while. But that was before their awkward meeting on the steps earlier. "If not, I can totally reschedule."

"Don't reschedule. I know how important the swim team is to you." He shrugged. "Plus, if anyone knows a thing or two about strategy, it's the Abdominator."

Immediately reassured and silently vowing to make it up to him later, when they were alone, Maggie reached up and gave him a quick hug.

"You two are cute, but love isn't going to save the swim team," Aimee called from the car. "Every second wasted is another signature lost!"

Maggie bit her bottom lip to keep from smiling as Arnie saluted Aimee and started marching down the steps. She was glad she did, too, because it was clear as soon as they climbed in the car that Aimee wasn't in a joking mood. Neither was Mrs. McDougall, who drove without speaking after her initial hello. Maggie expected Aimee to whip out notebooks and the petition right away to avoid wasting another second and losing another signature, but she simply stared straight ahead for the entire trip. Maggie would've preferred spending that time talking and joking with Arnie, but was afraid of fueling the fire that burned quietly in the front seat. She settled for holding his hand and sneaking him quick glances every few minutes.

After fifteen long minutes, they pulled up in front of Bananarama.

"Thank you for the ride, Mrs. McDougall," Maggie said politely before sliding out of the back seat.

"Yeah, thanks," Arnie added, sliding out after her.

"Later." Aimee jumped out of the front seat and slammed the passenger side door shut.

"Aimee, remember what we discussed."

Maggie stood next to Aimee as Mrs. McDougall leaned across the front seat and called out the open window.

"I expect you home in an hour. *One* hour. Sixty minutes."

"I do remember what we discussed," Aimee shot back coolly. "Including the fact that Maggie and I have a *lot* of work to do. I'll try to be home in an hour, but I wouldn't hold your breath. We'll probably be here all night."

Maggie's mouth fell open as Aimee spun on one heel and stomped into Bananarama, and the car sped away.

"Sorry about that," Aimee said as soon as Maggie and Arnie joined her at the smoothie counter inside. "You wouldn't believe the fight we had this morning. Unreal. And she doesn't seem to get that she's not the only with problems, you know? I mean, fifteen girls will be devastated forever if we don't save the swim team, and she's worried about whether I'm home for dinner? Please."

"That's awful." Maggie tried to catch Arnie's eye, but he was suddenly very interested in the fruity flavors lining the chalkboard overhead. "But, Aim, Arnie and I kind of have—"

"I know." Aimee frowned at Maggie. "You have a date. And I don't want to get in the way of true love. If anyone has a shot at the real thing, it's you two. But, Mags . . . I could really use a break. Just for tonight."

Maggie opened her mouth to suggest that they hang out for an hour then and maybe meet up later, after part two of Maggie's and Arnie's date, but Aimee turned back to the counter and started placing her order like there was nothing left to discuss. Maggie looked at Arnie again, but he was still staring intently at the chalkboard.

Maggie felt terrible. She felt terrible for Aimee, who was obviously upset. She felt terrible for Arnie, who clearly felt like the third wheel on what should've been a two-wheel ride. She felt terrible that they probably weren't going to make it to the lake, and that Operation First Kiss would be delayed. And worst of all, she felt terrible that she and Arnie were exactly where they were almost two hours before, when they stood awkwardly on the elementary school steps.

"I'm sorry," she whispered after she and Arnie had gotten their smoothies and headed toward the table Aimee had already taken over. "This wasn't part of the plan."

"No worries." He didn't look at her once as he dropped into a chair, sipped his smoothie, and turned the petition clipboard toward him. "Okay, so—swim team strategy. What do we have so far?"

14.

"Here you are, my lovely," Maggie's dad said, placing a ceramic mug on the coffee table. "Two teabags and one teaspoon of honey, just the way you like."

"Thank you, dear." Maggie's mom reached for the cup.

"Do you guys want some macaroni with that cheese?" Summer teased.

"I don't think macaroni and cheese is really a suitable tea accompaniment," her dad said thoughtfully. "Do you, my sweet?"

"Cream cheese, maybe," Maggie's mom said, tilting her head as she pretended to consider it. "On a whole-grain bagel or watercress sandwich. But definitely not cheddar. And definitely not with elbow-shaped pasta."

"Although . . ." Her dad smiled at her mom. "If that was

what my beautiful bride wanted, I'd whip up a batch right now."

"Wow. If you see our real parents, please let them know we're ready for them to come back," Maggie said, hiding her smile behind her computer screen. She and Summer liked to poke fun at their parents whenever they started being especially mushy together, but they also enjoyed seeing them so close. This time last year, when her dad wasn't working and her mom was stressed about money, the biggest display of affection they shared was when her dad asked her mom to pass the salt at the dinner table. So now, even though they sometimes laid on the cheese extra thick, Maggie and Summer wouldn't have wanted it any other way.

As her dad went to answer the telephone ringing in the kitchen, her mom cradled the mug in both hands, and Summer loaded the DVD player with that night's Netflix pick, Maggie returned to her history report. She didn't want to miss the family movie, but she still had a lot to do for the report, which was due the next day. The plan was to listen to *Willy Wonka and the Chocolate Factory* and comment accordingly while reviewing and organizing her notes.

"It's for you, Mag Pie."

"One second." Maggie's fingertips moved even faster across the keyboard as she hurried to finish her thought.

"I can take a message," her dad offered. "Or perhaps you'd like me to hold the phone to your ear so you can talk and type at the same time."

"Would you?" she asked hopefully, though she was pretty sure he was kidding.

She pouted as he patted her head and handed her the phone.

"What's up, buttercup?"

Maggie smiled instantly at the sound of Arnie's voice. They hadn't spoken since leaving Bananarama the day before, and she hadn't been sure when they'd talk again, since he was spending the day with his parents at their country club. And also because she wasn't sure if he was still unhappy about their dream team accidentally acquiring another member.

"Buttercup? You've clearly been spending too much time with my parents," she joked.

"There's no such thing," her dad said. He lifted her mom's feet from the couch so he could sit down, placed her feet in his lap, and started massaging her arches.

"Speaking of your family," Arnie said, "I know you're supposed to watch a movie with them tonight, and I don't want to interrupt your plans, but something came up that I just had to run by you."

"If you're taking your David Blaine act to Vegas, I'm there."

"Not yet, but I appreciate the support." He took a deep breath. "So, there's this thing at my parents' country club. It's an awards ceremony, and it's kind of a big deal—think chandeliers, tuxedoes, and enough champagne to swim in."

"Sounds fancy." Maggie's pulse quickened at what she hoped was coming.

"It is. You know I prefer chips to caviar, but I actually like this party. There's live music and really good food, and because of the champagne factor, even the stuffiest, crankiest adults—like Ma and Pa Gunderson—have fun."

"That's great." Maggie stared at the cursor on her computer screen and held her breath.

"It is . . ."

Please . . . please . . . please . . . , she silently pleaded with each blink of the cursor.

"So . . . do you think you'd want to go?"

"Yes." The word burst from her mouth like helium from a balloon. Aware of her family's curious looks, she stood up and balanced her computer carefully on one arm as she headed for the kitchen.

"Great," he exhaled. "I'm sorry it's such short notice. I would've asked sooner, but my parents were supposed to go with another couple, and that couple just bailed, like, fifteen minutes ago. And my mom dropped a hundred dollars on each ticket and would rather have a root canal than let that money go to waste, so she asked if you and I would like to use the extra tickets."

"Absolutely." Maggie sat in a chair at the kitchen table and opened her schedule spreadsheet. "And no problem about the short notice. Believe me—I'll find time. When is it?"

Arnie paused. "In an hour?"

Her heart slid to her stomach. "An hour? As in, an hour *tonight*, and not in an hour this time tomorrow? Or next week?" A party like the one Arnie described would probably make Operation First Kiss completely unnecessary. They were sure to be so mesmerized by the romantic atmosphere as they danced to live music under a sparkly chandelier surrounded by other couples in gowns and tuxedoes that kissing would came as naturally as breathing. Plus, how could she turn him down now when he'd patiently sat through four hours of swim team strategy at Bananarama the day before?

"I know that doesn't give you much time," he said.

She frowned at her schedule. It was jam-packed until ten o'clock that night, and picked up again at six o'clock the next morning. Scrolling ahead, she saw that she wasn't supposed to see Arnie again for three more days. That was a long time to worry about how awkward things would be on their next date.

"Well," she said, quickly typing "*Willy Wonka* recap/history report review" in the five a.m. spreadsheet square, "eight hours of sleep always seemed like a few too many to me."

"Awesome. My parents have to get there early because my dad's being honored, so we're all leaving in a few minutes, but we'll send the limo to pick you up after it drops us off."

"The limo?" Maggie could see her grin growing in her reflection on the computer screen.

"It's going to be amazing, Mags. See you soon."

Maggie hung up, saved and closed the spreadsheet, and flew from the kitchen. She slowed when she entered the living room and saw the movie's opening credits rolling on the TV, and looked away so she could try to get through this part relatively guilt-free.

"Mom, you know what you said the other day about daydreaming? And how I should be doing more of it?"

"Of course." Her mom smiled, apparently happy that Maggie had been listening.

"You were right. I think I definitely need to daydream more. Starting tonight."

"Don't they call it *day*dreaming for a reason?" Summer asked, nodding toward the darkening sky visible through the living room windows.

Maggie sat on the edge of the coffee table so that she was level with her mom. "There's a party at the Gundersons' country club. It's very formal and fancy, and if I go, a real limo will take me there. I know we're supposed to watch a movie tonight, but I thought maybe I could get up when you do tomorrow morning so we can talk about what I missed over an early breakfast?"

"Well, sure, Mag Pie . . . but don't you also have a lot of homework to do?"

"Yes." Maggie knew her mom didn't mention this because she worried Maggie wouldn't finish what she needed to, but because she worried *Maggie* would worry about not finishing what she needed to. "But this party will be better than anything I could ever imagine myself. It's a chance to make up for all the daydreaming I've missed out on so far. The homework will be there when I get back."

Her mom smiled at her dad, who took her mom's hand and kissed it. "Come on, Cinderella. I have the perfect dress."

Maggie jumped up and she, her mom, and Summer hurried down the hall toward her parents' room. They talked and laughed as Maggie got ready, and by the time the limo driver rang the doorbell an hour later, she'd managed to nudge all thoughts of homework, school, and other obligations to the very back of her brain. Because she was pretty sure most princesses weren't thinking about their history reports as they waited for their horse-and-carriages to arrive.

At exactly seven o'clock, Maggie stepped out of the limo and onto the long walkway leading to the front doors of the Paradise Cove Country Club. She couldn't wait to go inside and see Arnie, but standing there in her mom's sleeveless black velvet dress with a puffy skirt and sparkly rhinestone hem, the pearl necklace Aunt Violetta had given her for her twelfth birthday, and her favorite pair of black patent leather (one-inch) heels, she felt like something big was about to happen. Something major. Something that only happened once in a person's lifetime. She wanted to take an extra minute to memorize everything so that she would always remember the last moments leading up to the one moment that changed her life forever.

"Wow."

Maggie looked away from the white lights glittering in

the trees lining the walkway. She'd been so busy memorizing, she hadn't noticed the front doors open.

She stayed where she was as Arnie walked toward her. Her heart fluttered in her chest as she took in his black tuxedo, red bowtie, and matching vest. "Wow, yourself." He always looked great in his regular ensemble of cargo pants and a polo shirt, but he looked so adorable dressed up, Maggie thought she might suggest that they occasionally wear formal attire just for fun.

"*You* look amazing."

Feeling a warm flush spread across her face, Maggie looked down at the toes of her shiny black shoes. She loved Arnie's compliments but was still getting used to them. And thanks to their current surroundings—and the fact that he looked at her almost like he was seeing her for the first time—that one made her blush particularly quickly.

"Only because I'm standing next to you," she said, and then immediately worried that that was too much.

"Maggie . . ."

She swallowed. He stood so close, she could see the toes of *his* shiny black shoes two inches away from hers. Was this it? Was it going to happen right here, before they'd even walked through the front doors? Wasn't this too soon? Shouldn't they wait until the end of the night, after they'd

Maggie Bean in Love

eaten and danced and were too tired to be nervous? Or did none of that matter? Since he was Arnie and she was Maggie, and the first kiss would be perfect, just because it was theirs?

Deciding that was it, she raised her eyes and offered a small smile.

"Yes?"

He took another step toward her. She stopped breathing as her heartbeat drummed in her ears. She pressed her lips together to make sure the pink gloss was spread evenly, and noted the muffled jazz music coming from inside, the light wind lifting her bangs from her forehead, and the tiny white dot of dried toothpaste on Arnie's chin. These were the things she'd want to remember later, the details she'd want to tell Aimee, her future children, and her children's children.

"I couldn't *wait* . . ."

She shivered as he spoke near her ear. This was it. This was really going to happen. She, Maggie Bean, former chocoholic and current girlfriend to Arnie Gunderson, was finally going to do what only a year ago she'd thought impossible.

She was going to kiss a boy.

"I was counting down the *minutes* . . . until I could give you this."

Tricia Rayburn

She kept her eyes closed as she waited for his mouth to press against hers. When nothing happened, she lifted her chin, just in case he wasn't sure she was ready. When nothing happened again—and when she could smell blueberries and sugar mixing in the crisp fall air—she opened one eye, and then the other.

✎ "Crepes," he whispered.

"Crepes?" She eyed the white cloth napkin filled with gooey pastry he held in front of her face.

"They're like miniature pancakes filled with fruit, chocolate—whatever you want. They're amazing, and they apparently go really well with champagne. I grabbed this one for you right before the adults started licking the empty tray."

"Oh." She took the cloth napkin and fought a frown as a light dusting of powdered sugar landed on her mom's black velvet dress. "That's great. Thanks."

"Have you ever had one?"

She shook her head and smiled. He looked so proud of his preparty present she didn't want to let her disappointment show. Plus, it was only seven o'clock. Her curfew was ten, not midnight, but a determined Cinderella could still get her prince to kiss her in three hours.

So as the muffled jazz music streamed outside and the

wind lifted her bangs from her forehead, Maggie licked her lips, opened her mouth, and had her very first . . . crepe.

Whatever happened the rest of the night, this was one moment she would never forget.

15.

"Do you think Ms. P would notice if I started using the window instead of the door to get to history class?"

"Absolutely," Aimee said. "Our lovelorn gym teacher is zeroing in on every unsuspecting target she can find. Who knew that up until this year she'd been in a *good* mood?"

Maggie leaned against the wall next to their history classroom door and watched Anabel and Julia kiss their boyfriends like they all would never see one another again once the bell rang. "They have math this period, which is three hallways down, and their lockers are on the other side of the building." She pouted at Aimee. "It's like they know."

"They don't know," Aimee promised. "Even if they did, their agenda is much bigger than rubbing in the fact that they have boyfriends."

"That's *part* of their agenda. It's psychological warfare. They're taking advantage of my weakened emotional defenses to distract me from saving the swim team."

Aimee raised her eyebrows and nodded to the travel coffee mug Maggie held. "How many of those have you had today?"

"Not enough." Sighing, Maggie held the travel mug to one side of her face as she passed the happy couples and entered the classroom.

"I didn't know you were a coffee drinker," Aimee said as she and Maggie sat at their desks.

"I am as of last night. I still had homework to do when I got home from the party, and needed it to stay awake. Then when I finally went to bed, I was so wired from the caffeine that I couldn't sleep. So I just laid there, awake and depressed, until my alarm went off at five."

"And then you needed more to stay awake since you didn't get any sleep?" Aimee guessed.

"You got it." Maggie took a sip and winced. "It's terrible, by the way. I don't know how people do this every day."

"Mags, I know this will probably sound totally crazy . . . but have you considered talking to Arnie about things?"

"What's there to talk about? He says he likes me, but he obviously doesn't *like* me, like me. If he did, he'd want to kiss me. What teenage boy doesn't want to kiss his girl-friend?"

"Kissing usually goes with the territory," Aimee agreed. "But there are no rules for this kind of thing. There's no definite timeline. And you can't compare your relationship to the saliva-suckers we just saw in the hallway."

"I guess," Maggie said, sliding down her seat and hugging the travel coffee mug to her chest. After lying in bed and worrying all night about why Arnie hadn't kissed her on her doorstep after having a great time at the country club party, she'd hoped school would help take her mind off of things. It hadn't yet. "Anyway, how was the rest of your weekend? I'm guessing your mom wasn't happy that you weren't home for dinner the other night."

"Actually, I don't think she noticed." Aimee had been leaning toward Maggie but sat back and started pulling books from her backpack as soon as her mom was mentioned. "She and my dad were too busy having a heated discussion about who should get to stay in the house to notice. That's what they're calling their fights, now, by the way—*heated discussions.*"

Maggie frowned. According to her schedule, they had thirteen days left until the school board meeting. That meant Aimee had thirteen days left before she had to choose between living with her mom or dad. And besides referring to their arguments and needing to get out of the house, Aimee hadn't said one word about her deadline. Maggie didn't want to push Aimee to talk about anything she didn't want to—and she knew better than anyone that sometimes it was easier to pretend the problem didn't exist rather than face it—but she was worried for her friend.

"Aim," she said gently, "I know this will probably sound totally crazy, but have you considered talking to them about things?"

"What's there to talk about?" Aimee borrowed Maggie's response just like Maggie had borrowed Aimee's question. "They say they love me, but they obviously don't *love* me, love me. If they did, they wouldn't make me—"

Maggie had never disliked Ms. Pinkerton's whistle more as it blasted through the classroom—and stopped Aimee from admitting for the first time what it was her parents were making her do.

"Listen up, rabble-rousers." Ms. Pinkerton dropped into Miss Wells's chair, clasped her hands behind her head, and propped the heels of her white leather boots—which complemented a pair of royal blue cropped pants and an orange tank top—on the desk. "I interrupt your regularly scheduled programming to bring you the following special presentation."

Maggie sat up in her seat, suddenly feeling more awake. Special presentations, which usually came in the form of documentaries or guest speakers, were always good for catching up on other schoolwork. Teachers liked to take advantage of the time off to nap in the back of the room, and since the brim of Ms. Pinkerton's Yankees baseball hat was already lowered over her eyes, Maggie guessed she planned to do the same. That meant Maggie had just won forty-five extra minutes to read over her history report and pass a few notes with Aimee.

Not wanting the noise to invite any attention to her after the presentation had started, Maggie opened her spiral notebook and ripped out three pages. She was about to tear out a fourth when her classmates started whispering around her.

"Thank you, Ms. Pinkerton, for that lovely introduction. You're too kind."

Maggie's head shot up.

"What are *they* doing here?" Aimee whispered.

"And thank *you*, children," Mrs. Swanson continued before Maggie could answer. "We appreciate you taking a few minutes out of your busy days to learn about a very important cause. I hope you'll accept these small gifts as tokens of our appreciation."

"No, thanks," Maggie said when Mrs. Richards headed

Maggie Bean in Love

down the aisle between hers and Aimee's desks and offered a small silver basket wrapped in iridescent cellophane.

"Brownies, Red Bull, a Water Wings reusable water bottle, and fifteen more iTunes." Aimee stared at the contents of her basket, which she'd quickly emptied onto her desk. "Unbelievable."

Maggie faced the front of the classroom where Mrs. Swanson was perched on Miss Wells's desk. She wore gray, wide-legged wool pants, a silver silk blouse, and a gray cardigan that had to be cashmere. Mrs. Swanson might've been a mom, but she was still cool. And that wasn't going to help the swim team's cause.

"What is Ms. P *thinking*?" Maggie hissed to Aimee. "She coaches the swim team. How could she let them invade her classroom like this?"

"Maybe because it's not really *her* classroom?" Aimee shook her head, like it was the only explanation she could think of.

Maggie looked at Ms. Pinkerton, whose face was now completely hidden by the Yankees baseball hat. If she had a problem with the Water Wings mothers pushing their unfair, overpriced propaganda, she obviously didn't plan to do anything about it then.

"Now, as most of you have probably heard," Mrs.

Swanson said once Mrs. Richards had finished distributing the baskets and joined her on the desk, "the Water Wings are in a bit of trouble. And they really need your help."

"We'd like you to think of all the times the Water Wings have been there for *you*," Mrs. Richards added. She clicked the remote control she held and the picture of the silver wings gave way to a shot of the Water Wings marching in last year's Veterans Day parade.

"They can't be serious," Aimee whispered. "Are they serious?"

Maggie was too shocked by the image of the silver-suited girls marching with khaki-suited veterans to answer. She remembered that parade. The Water Wings had served as symbols of youthful support while the swim team had volunteered to build the float that carried Frank Merchant, the oldest living war veteran in their town.

"The Water Wings aren't just pretty girls in pretty swimsuits," Mrs. Swanson added. "They're not just about putting on a show. They're about helping others, and bringing a close-knit community even closer."

Maggie swallowed a groan when the parade picture was replaced by one of Julia and Anabel smiling into the camera as they stood by a Christmas tree and handed presents to children in pajamas. Maggie remembered that, too. Last year, the swim team had banded together with the baseball and soccer teams to collect toys for children spending the holidays in hospitals. They'd spent a month collecting more than two hundred toys—which the Water Wings had spent an hour handing out.

"The Water Wings understand the responsibility that comes with being the pillars that keep your school standing," Mrs. Swanson said. "They embrace this power and work tirelessly to put it to good use."

"Pillars?" Maggie repeated as another picture of Julia and Anabel appeared. This one featured the Water Wings cocaptains actually looking away from the camera as they sat in the front row of a school board meeting.

"They might want to stop buying iTunes and invest in a better graphic designer," Aimee said.

Maggie couldn't help but smile. She'd been too annoyed to catch it, but Aimee was right. The school board meeting in thirteen days would be the first the Water Wings attended. In the picture before them, Julia and Anabel wore shorts and T-shirts while everyone else was bundled up in corduroys and down coats. They'd been Photoshopped in to make it look like they were sitting in the front row and listening attentively to the principal.

"They'll listen to your needs and fight for what you want.

With your support, they'll continue to support you." Mrs. Richards clicked the remote control again, and a posed picture of Anabel offering to carry Julia's books appeared. "And in addition to making sure your concerns are heard, they'll make sure you enjoy school more than you ever have before."

Maggie scanned the room as Mrs. Swanson turned off the light and Mrs. Richards turned on an iPod with portable speakers. Her stomach flip-flopped when she saw that each and every one of her classmates was completely engaged in the special presentation. Most were even smiling. The only other times they looked so happy in history class was in the dead of winter, when heavy snowfalls led to early dismissals and they were minutes away from unexpected freedom.

"Free Frappuccinos," Mrs. Richards called out over the loud techno beats as a picture of Anabel and Julia holding frosty coffee drinks took over the screen. "If the Water Wings continue, you'll find a Starbucks van in the school parking lot every Monday morning. The Water Wings will hand out complimentary beverages to help jumpstart your week."

Maggie glanced at Aimee. Her lips were pressed so tightly together, Maggie could see them turning white, even in the darkened room.

"Free iTunes," Mrs. Swanson announced next. "We hope

you're all enjoying some new music this week. If you help the Water Wings, the Water Wings will help your playlist stay fresh. Every time report cards are issued, you'll receive more free iTunes—one song for every B, and five for every A."

Unfortunately, Maggie's classmates were buying it. They even joined Mrs. Richards when she started clapping.

"Lastly," Mrs. Swanson continued, "the Water Wings understand that school can be tough, and that you all deserve a fun chance to recharge every now and then."

"*Pool* parties?" one of Maggie's classmates declared.

Maggie couldn't stop her groan as another Photoshopped picture appeared on the screen. The real picture featured all of the Water Wings team members hanging out in the school pool in their silver swimsuits. Superimposed were images of their classmates, jumping off the diving board, drinking Frappuccinos while floating on rubber rafts, and dancing on the steps. Their heads were last year's yearbook portraits, and their bodies were borrowed from magazines.

"Is that me?" she asked Aimee, not bothering to whisper since the music was still pumping and everyone else was cheering. "Doing a cannonball into the shallow end?"

"Afraid so," Aimee said, squinting to make sure. "If it's any consolation, I'm all the way at the edge of the picture, collecting empty plastic cups."

"Once a month your Water Wings will use their practice time to throw a school-wide poolside bash," Mrs. Richards called out over the noise. "There will be music, dancing, eating, laughing, and, of course, swimming."

"All we ask is that you sign this petition now, and show up later," Mrs. Swanson said, raising a silver clipboard framed in glittery rhinestones. "The Water Wings—*your* Water Wings—will do the rest."

Maggie sank in her seat. As the unofficially official swim team leader, she thought she should probably try to defend their cause, but she didn't know how. She could point out that the Water Wings hadn't helped build Frank Merchant's parade float, or collect toys for sick children, or fight the school board on behalf of the student body . . . but what was the point? How could the truth compete with free Frappuccinos, iTunes, and pool parties? And why should she risk looking like the bad guy by trying to take those things away from her classmates when Ms. Pinkerton, the *real* swim team leader, was completely oblivious and snoring like a lawn mower?

Even Aimee, who'd voluntarily led the charge up until now, looked more sad than angry. "There are six hundred kids in school," she said. "We have a hundred and three signatures."

Maggie nodded, understanding the implication. After more than two weeks of trying to spread the word, they had the support of only half their own class. And that was support they'd gotten *before* the Water Wings announced their plans for an entire year of bribery. It wasn't looking good.

But as her classmates ate their brownies, drank their Red Bull, and gathered around the petition, Maggie thought that maybe it wasn't the worst thing in the world. She was already pressed for time *without* daily practices and regular meets. She couldn't imagine trying to find ten more hours in her schedule every week. And she was tired. Not just today, because of her sleepless night, but in general. She was so determined to be the best student, leader, daughter, friend, and girlfriend she could be, she didn't let herself *feel* tired very often. But the truth was, she would've loved to switch places with Ms. Pinkerton. She would've loved to take a nap in the middle of the day, just because there was nothing more pressing to do. And she could still swim without a team—she'd just have to do so when she and the pool were both free at the same time.

Which was why when Aimee pulled out the petition as they left the class at the end of the period, Maggie asked her to put it away.

"What's wrong?" Aimee's voice was tense. "I know it

seems impossible, Mags—I got overwhelmed in there too—but we still have time. We can't give up."

"Give up what?"

Maggie gripped her travel coffee mug and closed her eyes at the sound of the voice behind her. She usually didn't mind Carla popping up without warning, but now wasn't a good time.

"The swim team," Maggie said flatly, turning around. She shrugged as Carla's face fell. "They won. It's done."

16. Four days after the history class "special presentation," Maggie and Aimee sat cross-legged on her bed, surrounded by notebooks, textbooks, and highlighters.

Maggie had invited Aimee over to work on their reports, but hoped that after a few hours together Aimee would finally talk about what was going on with her parents. There were only nine days left before Aimee had to make her decision, and Maggie knew she was starting to panic. Maggie knew this not because of anything Aimee said or didn't say about her parents . . . but because she wouldn't stop talking about the swim team.

"What about mixes?" Aimee asked, pulling a stack of CDs from her backpack. "We can import all of these into your computer and pick and choose songs to make themed playlists. The possibilities are endless. We can do one for studying, one for exercising, one for riding the bus, whatever. I have, like, hundreds of blank CDs at home, so it wouldn't cost us anything."

"Except time," Maggie said. "Sorting through all those songs to find the right ones to ride the bus to could take hours. Then we'd have to burn the CDs, label them, and hand them out."

"I'll do it." Aimee's eyes were bright as she sat up straight. "I'll do it all. I have time. I don't mind."

Maggie frowned. "There's also the fact that everyone at school already has at least thirty free iTunes. They can download their own songs and make their own themed playlists. We'd still be the runner-up."

Aimee's shoulders slouched as she looked down at her notebook. "How about a bake sale? Or a yard sale? We can sell stuff to make money to help lower the cost of keeping the pool open."

"The Water Wings already gave out free brownies, so I doubt anyone would pay for ours. And my family had a yard sale before moving into this house. Do you know how much we made?"

Aimee tilted her head as she tried to calculate the monetary value of the old belongings of a family of four.

"A thousand? Two thousand?"

"Eighty-three dollars. And that was after ten hours of tough negotiations."

"What if we gave out brownies and mix CDs *at* the yard sale? We could advertise the freebies, which would attract people who wouldn't normally come, and then once we got them there, we could use our wit and charm to convince them to buy stuff."

"Aim, your wit and charm are powerful weapons, but I don't know if they're enough to convince people to buy our old clothes and toys."

Maggie watched Aimee flip forward a few pages in her notebook. She was frustrated, but unwilling to give up. Maggie wanted to let her talk about things on her own, and was beginning to worry that that wasn't going to happen. Part of her wanted to relent and agree to Aimee's suggestions— not because she thought they could still save the swim team, but because she wanted Aimee to be happy—but a bigger part knew that would only make things harder. The longer Aimee avoided the decision, the less time she'd have to think about it, and the tougher it would be to make it.

"I've got it!" Aimee's voice was triumphant as she tapped a pen on her notebook. "This is perfect. What if we—"

"Aim."

"Mags, this is the best idea yet. We just need to—"

"Aim," Maggie tried again, louder.

"I know you said you were done fighting, and I know some of the other ideas were kind of lame. But *this* one, Mags, this one is—"

"Aimee."

She stopped tapping the notebook and looked up. "What?"

Maggie pushed her history textbook to the side and scooted down the bed. "I appreciate everything you've done for the swim team. I really do. Without you, we never would've gotten the hundred and three signatures we did. We probably wouldn't have even had a petition."

Aimee shrugged and offered a small smile. "I'm happy to help. That's what best friends do."

That's what best friends do. Maggie hoped she remembered that when Maggie said what she was about to say.

"Aim, I know," Maggie said gently. "I know about your parents."

"My parents?" Aimee shook her head, confused by the sudden topic change. "Of course know you about them. So does your family. So does anyone living within a fifty-mile radius of my house. I'm pretty sure that's how far away you can hear them yelling."

Maggie's eyes held Aimee's. "I mean I know what happens in nine days. I know about the decision you have to make."

Aimee's blue-green eyes widened. After a second, she looked away and started gathering her books and highlighters on the bed. "If you've given up, that's fine—but there are still fourteen other girls who want to keep swimming. I'm sure they'd love to hear my ideas."

Maggie reached forward and grabbed Aimee's hand. "Like I said," she continued, her voice steady, "I'm very grateful for everything you've done. But . . . you're not even on the swim team."

"So?" Aimee stared at Maggie's hand on top of her own.

"*So* . . . I know you want to help, but I think you also might be focusing on the swim team to keep from focusing on what's going on at home."

"Of course you do." Aimee tugged her hand free and started shoving books in her backpack. "And that makes it the truth, right? If *Maggie* thinks that's what's going on, then that must be what's going on."

Maggie sat back. She'd expected reluctance, maybe a little resistance—but she hadn't expected an attack.

"How do you know, anyway?" Aimee stopped filling her backpack and looked at Maggie. "How did you find out? Did my mom tell yours?"

Maggie suddenly wished that *was* how she'd found out. As annoyed as Aimee sounded by the idea of her mother talking about their private family issues with other people, Maggie knew she was about to become even more upset.

"I saw it in your notebook," Maggie admitted. "A few weeks ago, when you were over here and went to the kitchen to get a snack. I just wanted to get a closer look at your swim team notes."

Aimee's fair skin slowly turned peach.

"I didn't mean to see it, I promise," Maggie said quickly. "It was just there. And since you didn't tell me what was going on your own, I figured you just weren't ready to talk about it. I wanted to wait until you brought it up."

Aimee zipped her backpack and slid off the bed.

"We talk about everything," Maggie said, jumping to her feet. "That's what we do. And I thought we should talk about this before it was too late."

"Too late?" Aimee asked. "For who? You? Did you plan to bring this up tonight? Was this my square on your spreadsheet schedule?"

"That's not fair." Maggie *had* marked it on her spreadsheet, but only because she wanted to make sure they had enough time to talk about everything that needed to be talked about. "And I only keep a schedule to make sure everything gets done. It's hard to do, especially when people drop by without warning and change my plans."

Aimee's eyes narrowed. "You want to know what's not fair? Spending hours every day trying to help someone who only wanted to give up."

"What does that mean?" Maggie could hear the defensiveness in her voice. "You know I love the swim team. I agreed to be the leader, didn't I? Even though I had a million other things to do? I stood in the rain, and sat at that table every day, and talked to people I never talked to before, just so the swim team could go on."

"Yes, you sat at a table—to collect signatures for a petition *I* created."

"A petition you *insisted* on. I told you I didn't think that would be enough to convince the board that we deserved the pool more than the Water Wings did."

"You're right." Aimee nodded. "You did. What you *didn't* do was come up with a better idea. Even Brainless and Babbling Barbie came up with Frappuccinos and pool parties."

"Excuse *me* for not wanting to stoop to bribery," Maggie said, her cheeks burning. "And maybe I did give up. But at least I didn't win by buying people off."

"Well, congratulations. Now you'll have oodles of extra

time to stare at your computer screen and plan your life instead of living it."

Maggie's chin dropped. Aimee's face softened slightly, as if for just a second she wanted to take back what she'd said, but then she raised her eyebrows without speaking or looking away. They probably would've stood like that for hours—both worked up and neither wanting to be the first to give—if Maggie's mom hadn't poked her head into the room right then.

"Maggie?" she asked, peering around the edge of the open door. "Sorry to interrupt, but you have a visitor."

"Arnie?" Maggie glanced at Aimee as he hurried into the room. "Were we supposed to get together tonight?" Her heart thumped in her chest. Had she double-booked?

"Nope." He smiled at her, then at Aimee. "And I know you're busy. I just wanted to give you a little something to keep you going in case you end up working late."

"Hot chocolate?" Maggie took the cardboard cup holder from him.

"And *Friends*." He crossed the room, placed a portable DVD player on her desk, and turned it on. "I thought maybe you could watch for a few minutes if you start to feel tired or stressed. Sometimes a good laugh is better than eight hours of sleep."

"Thanks," Maggie said, wondering if Aimee found Arnie's TV-show choice ironic too. "I'm sure it'll be very helpful."

"Great." He made sure the DVD worked and then paused it on the opening credits. "So, have fun, and don't work too hard. I'll talk to you later."

After Arnie said good-bye and disappeared into the hallway, Maggie's mom looked from Maggie to Aimee and back to Maggie. "I knocked, by the way. Three times."

Maggie looked at Aimee, but Aimee stared at the floor.

"Anyway, your father would like to invite you to this evening's viewing of *Charlotte's Web*."

"*Charlotte's Web?*" Maggie repeated.

"Like, the movie with all the talking animals?" Aimee asked. "And Julia Roberts as the spider?"

"Yes. I think it got very good reviews, and we—" Maggie's mother stopped talking and looked behind her. When she turned back, she was trying not to smile. "Forgive me. Tonight's selection is actually the original version of *Charlotte's Web*, which originally aired a long, long time ago and does not feature Julia Roberts in any way, shape, or form." She leaned further in the doorway and lowered her voice. "Your father just discovered the cartoon section on Netflix."

"Not *cartoons*," Maggie's dad called from the hallway. "Animated *films*."

Maggie's mom rolled her eyes playfully. "In any case, cookies and Charlotte are in the living room if you want them."

"That's nice," Aimee said quietly after the door was closed and they could hear Maggie's parents talking and laughing as they headed down the hallway. "The way Arnie tries to make you so happy. And the way your parents get along."

"It is." Maggie nodded. "Summer and I are still getting used to our parents, but it's definitely an improvement over last year, when . . ."

"When they were fighting?" Aimee finished.

Maggie didn't say anything. Aimee had brought it up, but Maggie didn't want it sound like she was rubbing in the fact that her parents were no longer fighting, since that was all Aimee's parents were doing.

Aimee dropped her backpack to the floor. "I'm sorry."

"Me too," Maggie said quickly, relief relaxing her muscles enough to step toward Aimee. "I didn't mean to snoop, or spy. And I brought it up only because I was worried about you."

"I know." Aimee sank to the floor. "The only reason I didn't bring it up first was because I didn't know what to say. I didn't even know where to start."

Maggie sat on the floor in front of Aimee. They were so close, their knees touched.

"I mean, I have a hard enough time picking out a pair of socks to wear every morning, and they expect me to pick one of them? Just like that?"

Maggie shook her head. She hadn't always gotten along with her dad, but even if her parents had decided to divorce during some of their worst times, she knew she still would've had a hard time choosing between them.

"And all I can do is wonder why they're putting this one on me. They decided to split up without asking for my opinion, so why the consideration now? Or is it not consideration? Do they just want someone else to make the decision for them?"

"I don't know," Maggie said truthfully. "But it doesn't seem fair."

Aimee looked down and absently played with her shoelaces. "It wasn't fair of me to push the petition, or all the meetings and planning. It wasn't fair of me to totally intrude on your date with Arnie."

"It's okay. I really was grateful for your help, and know we wouldn't have gotten that far without you." Maggie shrugged. "It just wasn't meant to be."

"Well, you were right. I was focusing on the swim team so I didn't have to focus on my parents." Aimee untied her shoelaces, retied them, and then looped them in a double-knot. "And I know I have to make this decision, I know that I only have nine days . . . but I don't know when I'll be ready to talk about it. I don't know if I'll *ever* be ready to talk about it."

Maggie reached forward and tugged on the shoelaces in Aimee's other sneaker until they came undone. "You know where to find me."

Smiling, Aimee started retying the shoelaces. "I do. Thanks."

"And in the *meantime*," Maggie said, bringing her legs to her chest and resting her chin on her knees, "if you need something else to focus on besides your parents—or your shoelaces—you can always help me move forward with Operation First Kiss."

"I'm ready for duty." Aimee saluted Maggie. "I still have twelve packs of index cards, three Post-it pads, and six brand-new highlighters to use. What's our next move?"

The next move was to plan the most perfect, romantic date any couple had ever been on . . . the kind of date that would make two people who were once very much in love fall head-over-heels all over again. Considering the lack of kissing, Maggie didn't think she and Arnie had reached the love stage—yet. But when they did, she wanted to make sure that nothing could pull them apart.

17. "Can I have a hint?"

"Nope." Cradling the phone between her ear and shoulder, Maggie grabbed a cookbook from the kitchen cabinet and added it to the pile on the counter.

"How about a *hint* of a hint?"

"I already told you that our next date is sure to be the best night of your entire life." Maggie grinned at Arnie's eagerness. "What more do you need to know?"

"What to wear, for one," Arnie said. "What if I show up in shorts and a T-shirt to go to the skating rink? I don't think the best night of my entire life involves me trying to stay upright while shivering on blades of steel."

"We're not going to the skating rink. And you can whatever you're comfortable in. You can even wear pajamas, if you want."

"Interesting . . . I *do* have a new pair of awesome slipper socks I've been dying to show off."

"Perfect."

"But there's also the issue of what time to show up. And where. And what I should bring."

"All you need to bring is yourself. I'll take care of the rest. And as for when and where, you'll find out soon enough."

Arnie paused. "Can I at least have a hint of a hint of when soon enough will be?"

"Try to think of it like Christmas morning, when the presents are piled under the tree." Maggie lifted the heavy stack of cookbooks, carried them across the kitchen, and placed them on the table next to four others she'd already looked at. "It's exciting because you know they're for you, but you have no idea what they are."

"I *always* know what my presents are. I send Santa a very long, very detailed list every year. And because I'm never naughty—and because Santa's usually very busy closing deals and attending business meetings and doesn't have much time to plan surprises—I always get everything I ask for."

"That's just sad," Maggie said, flipping through her mom's *Low-Sugar Showstoppers* cookbook. "And it makes me even more determined to keep the surprise a surprise."

"Fine." Arnie sighed. "It's a good thing I still have to come up with an Abdominator exercise for the website this week. If I didn't have that to keep me busy, I'd probably be calling every hour for updates."

"It *is* a good thing," Maggie agreed. "Because you could call every minute, and you still wouldn't get any updates."

"Well, no matter what, I know I'm going to have a great time."

"Me too," Maggie said, her smile growing.

After they said good-bye and hung up, Maggie flipped through the *Low-Sugar* cookbook in search of the perfect dessert to make for Arnie. She'd already found a recipe for the perfect dinner—chicken fajitas on whole-wheat tortillas with homemade salsa and guacamole—and the dessert had to be just as good. Because the meal was only the first part of the perfect night she'd planned for them, and she couldn't risk any part of it being anything *but* perfect.

As if seeing the plan would help her pick the meal's grand finale, she slid her laptop down the table until it pressed against the cookbook. She opened Maggie's Master Multi-Tasker, clicked on the Smooch tab, and reviewed the evening's goals and itinerary.

GOAL 1: Make up for any previous date awkwardness

GOAL 2: Make sure Arnie knows how much I like him

GOAL 3: First kiss

ITINERARY

4 p.m.: Bake dessert

5 p.m.: Start cooking dinner

5:30 p.m.: Get dressed

5:45 p.m.: Prepare appetizers

6 p.m.: Arnie arrives

6:10 p.m.: Eat appetizers

6:20 p.m.: Eat dinner

7 p.m.: Eat dessert

7:30 p.m.: Start entertainment

8 p.m.: Have meaningful conversation

8:30 p.m. (approx.): KISS

9 p.m.: Family returns, Arnie leaves

Maggie smiled at the computer screen. As soon as her mom had asked if Maggie would like to come with them to a birthday party for one of Summer's friends, she'd known it was the perfect opportunity for a romantic night with Arnie. She'd had to tell a tiny white lie to get her mom's permission to have Arnie over—which was that Aimee and Peter were coming over too—but it was a small price to pay for what the evening would bring. And, thanks to her careful planning, everything was coming together even better than she'd hoped. She'd already bought a new outfit and arranged the entertainment, so the only thing left to do before the big day was to try to not get nervous—and to find the perfect dessert.

She returned to the cookbook and scanned dozens of recipes. Nothing sounded quite right. Baked pears were too basic. Raspberry granitas were too slushy. Banana yogurt parfaits were too bland. Cinnamon oranges were too juicy. Strawberry angel food cake was too spongy. These desserts were so healthy, they could also be eaten for breakfast. Not only that, she and Arnie had already had caramel apples and blueberry crepes on previous dates, which, despite their thick sugar coatings, were still fruity if not exactly healthy desserts.

Those had been fine for those dates, but for *this* date, which was the one that all the others were leading to, she thought dessert should be something special. Something they'd never forget. Something . . . with chocolate. She'd never had a Valentine, but she'd certainly spent enough time in the drugstore candy aisle to know that boyfriends didn't give their girlfriends baked pears in celebration of their love every February fourteenth. They gave them chocolate. Boxes and boxes of chocolate.

She'd just closed *Low-Sugar Showstoppers* and was about to go online to look for more appropriate recipes when the phone rang.

She smiled as she picked up the cordless. "It's been fifteen minutes. Did you really think I'd cave so soon?"

"Maggie?"

Her smile disappeared. Unless Arnie's latest Abdominator exercise involved inhaling helium that raised his voice three octaves, he wasn't on the other end of the line. "Yes?"

"Oh, thank goodness." The woman exhaled loudly. "You have no idea how long this has taken. I thought I had your number written down on a piece of paper in my wallet, but my wallet was empty. Then I thought I might've put it in a shoebox with all my other important papers, but it wasn't there. Then I thought I must've put it on the refrigerator so that I had easy access to it at all times, but the only things on the refrigerator were expired coupons and pictures of Peabody."

"Peabody?" Maggie asked, now recognizing the voice—and the disorganization.

"My cat," Electra said. "*Anyway*, I finally found your number under the couch on your old Pound Patrollers index card, and I'm so glad I did."

"Electra," Maggie said gently, "I'd be happy to give you a lesson in spreadsheets sometime."

"Thanks, but I think I'll stick with my old-fashioned pen and paper. You can't get lazy working by hand."

Maggie frowned. Electra didn't sound like herself. In fact, she sounded almost annoyed. "What's wrong? Did something happen?"

"Yes, something happened." Electra sighed and groaned at the same time. "And Maggie, let me preface this by saying that I adore you. You know I think the world of you and Arnie, and I'm so proud of everything you've done for yourselves, and for Patrol This."

"Thank you . . . I think." Maggie's pulse quickened. If Electra felt the need to remind Maggie how she felt about her overall, then that meant there was something specific she wasn't happy with.

"So, remember last week, when we mailed out the Patrol This members' status updates? Their *confidential* updates, with personalized diet recommendations, exercise tips . . . and weights?"

"Of course." Maggie had taken on the responsibility herself and stayed up until two in the morning organizing, printing, and stuffing and labeling envelopes. The updates had needed to be mailed the following day in order to reach families in time for the next Patrol This meeting. "Did the parents not get them? The envelopes were pretty thick, but I made sure I had enough postage. I hope they didn't—"

"Every envelope went to the address on its label."

"Oh, thank goodness." Maggie's eyelids fluttered closed in relief.

"The problem was what was inside the envelopes."

Her eyes snapped open. "*Inside* the envelopes?"

"When I got home tonight, I had twenty-three messages. I didn't even know my voice mail could hold that many messages."

"What'd they say?" Maggie's voice was practically a whisper.

"Well, the first one was from Mrs. Marsh, Antonia's mom. Do you know Antonia?"

"Eight years old, blond hair, green eyes, missing top tooth," Maggie said automatically.

Electra paused. "Wow."

Maggie pulled her laptop toward her and opened the Patrol This spreadsheet. "She came in at eighty-seven pounds, and as of last week, was down to eighty-four."

"That's why Mrs. Marsh and Antonia were confused. The current weight on the paperwork they received was a hundred and sixty-three pounds."

"That doesn't make any sense," Maggie said. "The only member in the one sixties is Clint Baxter."

"Right. Mrs. Marsh and Antonia figured that out when they turned the page and saw Clint's name listed with all of his previous weights and measurements."

Maggie stopped breathing as the blood rushed to her cheeks.

"The next message was from Mr. London. He and his daughter, Natalie, received paperwork for Wendy Pong. The third message was from Mrs. Wilson, who received paperwork for Robbie Fitzpatrick."

"No," Maggie moaned. "No, no, no."

"I'm afraid so. All of the messages were to report receiving wrong paperwork. More important, the kids are devastated that their personal information is no longer confidential."

"Of *course* they are. I just don't understand how this happened." Maggie scrolled down the Patrol This spreadsheet for clues. "I'm so careful with their information. I always double- and triple-check anything I enter."

"Did you happen to double- and triple-check the envelope address labels against the paperwork inside?"

"Absolutely." Maggie shook her head. "I mean, I think so. I must have."

But the truth was, she couldn't remember. Right then, all she could recall about that night was that it had been very late, and she'd had three cups of coffee to make sure she stayed awake long enough to finish the project. She'd even been so sleepy at one point that she'd set her alarm and taken a fifteen-minute nap.

"Well, there's nothing we can do about it right now. I just wanted to give you a heads up in case they couldn't wait for me to call them back and tried calling you. Or in case they showed up at your door with torches and pitchforks."

Maggie swallowed. "You really think they're that mad?"

Electra sighed. "I think we'll have a pretty big fire to put out at the next meeting. It can be done, but not without some serious damage control."

"I'm sorry, Electra." Maggie blinked back tears when the computer screen grew blurry. "I'm so sorry. This isn't like me."

"I know, and it'll be okay. Just get some sleep and try not to worry. We'll figure it out tomorrow."

Maggie wasn't sure how long she sat at the kitchen table after hanging up the phone. She didn't look for recipes, update her schedule, or review her spreadsheets. She just sat there, staring at the computer without seeing it, and wondering how she could've been so careless. Mislabeling the envelopes was the kind of simple, silly mistake she hated to make—and worked tirelessly to avoid. And not only had she made the mistake, she'd done so at the expense of the Patrol This members' comfort and security. She couldn't have felt worse if she'd borrowed Ms. Pinkerton's megaphone, stood on the elementary school steps on a Monday morning, and blasted the kids' weights at the top of her lungs.

After a while, when she checked her watch and saw that it was almost midnight, she got up and made a pot of coffee. She'd been drinking several cups a day for almost two weeks, and the idea of drinking any more so late at night made her stomach turn . . . but she had no choice. Tomorrow, there would be fires to put out. And since she hadn't planned for fires, she had a lot of work to do before she could go to sleep.

18.

Maggie was so tired in history class the next day, she had to rest her chin on top of her travel coffee mug to keep from laying her head on the desk and falling asleep.

"Are you sure you don't want me to stay?" Aimee asked when the bell rang and Maggie didn't move.

"I'm sure." Maggie sighed, reached both arms overhead, and stretched, like she'd just woken from a nap. "But thanks."

"And you're *sure* this is what you want to do?"

Maggie looked at her. "Aim, it's already done. It's been done for weeks."

"Right." Aimee waited, as if Maggie might still change her mind. When Maggie didn't, Aimee stood up and handed her the clipboard. "Good luck."

"Thanks." Maggie took the clipboard and watched Aimee leave, suddenly feeling wide-awake.

With the school board meeting only a week away, Maggie had decided she'd better let Ms. Pinkerton know that the swim team might as well hang up their swimsuits for good. The plan was to show Ms. Pinkerton what they'd accomplished during the campaign and explain how that couldn't compete with free iTunes, Frappuccinos, and pool parties. If, after their conversation, Ms. Pinkerton wanted to rally the rest of the swim team to give it one last push, or if she still wanted Maggie to attend the school board meeting on their behalf, that was fine . . . but Maggie knew they'd only be wasting time. She also didn't think Ms. Pinkerton would care, considering she'd basically rolled out a red carpet for Mrs. Swanson and Mrs. Richards to trample them on the week before.

But now that they were alone in the classroom, Maggie was nervous. Ms. Pinkerton might not have supported their efforts as much as Maggie thought she would, but not long ago, she'd encouraged Maggie to join the swim team instead of accepting a belated, reluctant invitation to join the Water Wings. Maggie didn't know if she would've made it through seventh grade without the swim team, and she didn't know if she would've joined the swim team without Ms. Pinkerton's encouragement.

But not long ago was still a year ago. A lot had happened since then, and she wasn't the same person. She was thinner, stronger, and more confident. She even had a *boyfriend*, which she'd once hoped for but never thought possible. She didn't need the swim team the way she once had.

Assuring herself that this was just the last chapter of a great book that she didn't have to read every day in order to remember forever, Maggie stood up and walked toward the front of the classroom.

"Did you and your fellow brainiacs bug the joint?"

Maggie stopped two feet in front of Miss Wells's desk when Ms. Pinkerton spoke without looking up from the issue of *InStyle* she'd been reading all period. "What do you mean?"

Ms. Pinkerton yanked open a drawer, removed a tall stack of papers, and dropped it on the desk.

"What are those?" Maggie asked.

"Like you don't know," Ms. Pinkerton sniffed, returning to the magazine.

"I don't."

Ms. Pinkerton finished reading the caption underneath a full-page photo of Cameron Diaz before raising her eyes to Maggie. "You didn't install video cameras around the room?"

"What?" Maggie shook her head, taken aback by the accusation. "No. Why would I do that?"

Ms. Pinkerton nodded slowly, as if trying to decide whether Maggie could be believed. "What do you want, Bean?"

Still confused but now wanting to do what she needed to and get out of there as fast as possible, Maggie placed the clipboard on top of the magazine.

"What's this?"

"A petition," Maggie said, trying to keep her voice steady. "To save the swim team. We talked to tons of kids, and collected a hundred and three signatures."

Ms. Pinkerton flipped through the pages of names. "Not bad."

"Not great, either."

Ms. Pinkerton leaned back, crossed her arms over her chest, and peered at Maggie from underneath the brim of her baseball hat. "If you have something to say, Bean, say it."

Maggie stood up straight and squared her shoulders. This was it. She just had to say the words, and they could all move on.

"It's over," she blurted. "The swim team. It's over."

"What do you mean?" Ms. Pinkerton checked her watch. "The meeting's not for a week."

"Ms. P, let's face it," Maggie said, her heart thudding in her chest. "We can't compete with the Water Wings. We never could. We were done as soon as the board said it was us or them."

Ms. Pinkerton didn't say anything as her eyes narrowed.

"If you want to talk it over with the other girls, that's fine. And if you still want me to go to the meeting and present the petition, I will. But as the team's unofficial official leader, I have to say that I think it's a lost cause." Maggie paused for a response, but Ms. Pinkerton continued to stare at her without speaking. "I know you had to make us try, and I appreciate that—but I also know you feel the same way. If you didn't, you never would've let Anabel's and Julia's moms come in here and brag about their daughters for an entire period."

Maggie held her breath as Ms. Pinkerton looked down at the clipboard. Given her lack of interest up until now, Maggie expected her to shrug her shoulders, and maybe tell Maggie that it was her life and she didn't care one way or the other how Maggie chose to live it. Or, if she was having an even worse day than usual, Maggie was braced for a torrent of shouting, name slinging, and door slamming. But what Maggie *didn't* expect, what she couldn't have even imagined, was the response she actually got.

"Ms. P," she said quietly when Ms. Pinkerton's wide shoulders started to tremble, "are you crying?"

Ms. Pinkerton shook her head and sniffed.

"Yes, you are. The ink's running on the petition." Maggie stepped toward the desk. "What is it? What's wrong?"

"Nothing." Ms. Pinkerton took a deep breath, lifted her head like it weighed fifty pounds, and looked at Maggie. "It's just . . . you *love* the swim team."

Maggie's heart leaped when she saw the tears pooling in Ms. Pinkerton's eyes. "I do," she reassured her quickly. "I *did*. I'll always be grateful for everything it did for me. And if this year was like last year, I'd be at every practice and meet."

Ms. Pinkerton's tears spilled over. Her mascara ran in thin black lines down her cheeks.

"It was great while it lasted," Maggie continued, feeling like the adult as she took a box of tissues from the corner of Miss Wells's desk and offered it to Ms. Pinkerton. "But nothing lasts forever. At some point, we always have to move on . . . you know?"

Ms. Pinkerton snatched a tissue from the box and blew her nose so loudly, Maggie jumped. "Why?" she whimpered, her face crumpling. "Why do we have to move on? Who says?"

"Well . . . the school." Maggie wasn't sure what to make

of the unexpected response. Up until two minutes ago, she wouldn't have thought Ms. Pinkerton was physically capable of shedding a single tear—let alone crying over something that had seemed to annoy her more than it made her happy. "And the school's budget. It wasn't anything we did or didn't do. Our time was just up."

Ms. Pinkerton grabbed another tissue, and another, and another. "It's not fair," she whined, pawing at her eyes. "It's just not fair."

Maggie took the rest of the tissues out of the box and placed them on top of the petition. Ms. Pinkerton was crying so hard now, her shoulders shook instead of trembled, the chest of her silver sleeveless blouse was turning black from absorbing stray tears, and her breaths sounded like burp-hiccup hybrids. Maggie had never seen Ms. Pinkerton emotional without yelling, and she didn't know what do. She wanted to help, but worried about saying the wrong thing and making Ms. Pinkerton fall to the floor in hysterics.

As it was, she was already going to be late to English class.

"Like I said," she tentatively tried again, "you can talk to the rest of the girls. I'll still go to the school board meeting. We can—"

"No." Ms. Pinkerton honked into a ball of tissues. "You're right. What's the point?"

Maggie snuck a glance at the clock hanging over the closet. The second bell would ring in thirty seconds.

"We'll get through it," Ms. Pinkerton blubbered. "We'll pick up the scattered pieces of our shattered hearts, brush them off, try to glue them back together, and hope that some day, some way, they'll feel something again."

"Right . . ." Maggie watched the second hand tick toward the top of the clock. "Ms. P, I really don't want to leave you alone like this . . . but I kind of have to get to English. And I still have to go to my locker, which is on the other side of the building. I can come back at lunch if you want, or we can meet after school to finish talking, or—"

"No, no." Ms. Pinkerton inhaled a long, shaky breath. "I'll have to get used to it. Being alone, I mean."

Maggie nodded and started slowly backing toward the door. "I'm really sorry for upsetting you. I didn't mean to."

"I know." Ms. Pinkerton blew her nose, tossed the used tissue in the trash can by the desk, and wiped her palms on her shorts. "Bean, wait."

Maggie stopped just as the bell rang.

"Here." Ms. Pinkerton flipped through the stack of papers she'd pulled from the desk drawer. She pulled out a smaller pile from the middle of the stack and handed them to Maggie. "I thought this was what you wanted to talk about. Miss Wells stopped by this morning and dropped off your graded reports. She might be back for good next week so she asked me to hang on to them until then, but I know how you love your tests and papers. This might help when you're all alone in your bedroom later tonight, feeling sad, and lonely, and—"

"Thank you." Maggie took the papers without looking at them and hurried toward the door. "I'm sorry—I really have to go. We'll talk more later, I promise. Hang in there!"

Maggie darted through the door and dashed down the hallway, wondering what exactly had just happened. She'd assumed some of the swim team members might be sad about having to find another extracurricular activity, but she'd never thought Ms. Pinkerton cared enough to be so upset. She didn't have time to worry about it right then, though, because she was already more than a minute late to her next class and still had to get her English notebook from the other side of the building.

She was out of breath and fanning her maroon face by the time she reached her locker three minutes later. She dropped her backpack and papers to the floor, and spun the combination. Her fingers were slippery with perspiration and slid around the dial, making her overshoot the first number twice. When she landed on 35 instead of 36 for the third time, she groaned and tapped her forehead lightly against the locker door.

On the second tap, her eyes fell to the top page of the pile of papers Ms. Pinkerton had given her. She'd been so intent on getting out of the room, she hadn't bothered to see what they were. Now, even though the red words written in Miss Wells's neat handwriting were upside-down, Maggie could read them as if they were right-side-up and directly in front of her.

> Maggie—
> Decent effort, but not your best work. Let's meet after school and discuss.

When her eyes got to the last line, she reached down and grabbed the papers.

> Grade: C

"That's impossible," she whispered, her eyes locked on the single letter. "That has to be a mistake."

"Maggie?"

Thirty-six phone calls, twenty-four dates, thirty-six kisses.

She closed her eyes against the refrain that shot through her head. It was the same one she'd silently repeated every time she'd gone to her locker last year, when going to her locker wasn't just about exchanging books between classes.

"Are you okay?"

She opened her eyes, surprised when a single tear fell to the paper, making the ink run and the C grow. "Yes," she said brightly, grabbing her backpack from the floor.

"Good. I wasn't sure, since I hadn't seen you all month."

Maggie blinked back the other tears that threatened to fall. When she thought she could speak again without crying, she turned around. "Hi, Peter."

"Hi." He started to smile, but stopped when he saw that she obviously wasn't okay. "Maggie—"

"It's been a while, I know." Clutching her backpack straps in one hand and her history report in the other, she started shuffling backward. "We totally need to catch up. And we will—but not now. I can't right now."

He stepped toward her. "Wait, let's—"

"I have to get to English," she said, hoping she was far enough away that he couldn't see the thin streams rolling down her cheeks. "But we'll talk after next period, or maybe tomorrow!"

She spun around as soon as she turned the corner and sprinted down the hall, toward the girls' bathroom. Once inside the pink safe haven, she locked herself in the very last stall. She made sure the toilet lid was closed, sat down, and buried her face in her hands.

Maggie had never cut class before. She'd never mislabeled envelopes, or betrayed thirty kids. She'd never let someone else win without first giving everything she had, or consciously avoided a friend for four weeks straight. And she'd definitely never gotten a C.

She knew there was a first time for everything, but this was out of control.

19. "Nutley's Noodle Shack delivers, you know."

Maggie looked up from the cookbook to see her mom standing in the kitchen doorway.

"Don't your friends like wontons?" Maggie's mom asked. "Egg rolls? Fortune cookies?"

"Who doesn't like fortune cookies?" Maggie's dad peeked over her mom's shoulder. "Wow."

"I know it looks bad." Maggie scanned the kitchen. It actually looked like Rachael Ray had tangoed with the Tasmanian devil in the middle of the room. Pots and pans covered the counter. Avocados and tomatoes spilled out of plastic shopping bags and onto the table. Every cabinet and drawer was partially open. And flour and cocoa powder blanketed the tile floor. "But it'll be spotless by the time you get back. I promise."

"Sweetie," her mom said, stepping carefully around the patches of flour and cocoa powder, "it's very nice of you to make dinner for everyone . . . but isn't this a bit much?"

Maggie jumped when the oven timer dinged. She dashed to the stove, yanked open the oven door, and reached in with both hands to pull out the pan inside.

"Nutley's Noodle Shack *doesn't* deliver to the emergency room."

Maggie froze. Her eyes traveled from her bare hands, which were only inches away from burning metal, to the pink oven mitts her mom had just swatted her arm with. "Maybe the ambulance can swing by on the way?" she tried to joke, taking the mitts.

Apparently not wanting to distract her more, her mom waited for her to remove the pan and close the oven door before speaking again. "Maggie, is everything okay?"

"I'm not sure." She placed the pan on a metal cooling rack and examined the chocolate cakes. "Are they supposed to sink in the middle like that?"

"I wasn't referring to your dessert." Her mom stood next to her and leaned closer to the pan for a better look. "Though I don't think so."

Maggie turned away from the cakes and headed for the refrigerator so her mom couldn't see her face turn pink. She was already running behind schedule and wouldn't have time to bake another dessert if this one wasn't perfect, but she didn't want her mom to see her panic. As badly as things were going, they'd be much, much worse if her parents decided to stay home to make sure she didn't burn the place down.

"Everything's fine," Maggie said, grabbing a package of chicken from the refrigerator. "It's great."

"Okay . . ." Her mom watched her as she used a long, sharp knife to open the package and slice the chicken on a cutting board. "But we haven't see you much the past few days. And when we have, you haven't seemed quite like yourself."

Maggie forced the knife quickly through the meat. If she hadn't seemed like herself that was because she hadn't *felt* like herself. But that was all going to change—starting tonight.

"We have to go, people!" Summer called as she flew by the kitchen doorway. "There's going to be a magician! And a clown! And a Jonas Brothers cover band! We can't be late!"

Maggie looked up from the chicken. "You don't want to miss the Jonas Brothers cover band."

Her mom tilted her head. "You know you can talk to me about anything."

"I do," Maggie said, even though "anything" had

exceptions. Like cutting class. And practically failing history. And giving up on the swim team. And messing up the most important Patrol This mailing ever. And making sure she and Arnie had an amazing night so that he would finally kiss her and the rest of it would no longer matter.

"Good. Please remember that." Her mom kissed the top of her head and started out of the kitchen. "And also please remember to turn off the oven when you're done. And to load the dishwasher. And—"

"I will."

Her mom smiled, blew her another kiss, and disappeared through the doorway.

Maggie continued cutting chicken until she heard her dad's car start and drive away. Once they were gone, she dropped the knife to the counter and dashed back to the miniature chocolate cakes. They weren't perfect, but at least they'd stopped sinking. She'd just have to cover up the sagging centers with extra whipped cream.

Deciding that would have to do, since it was already 5:25 and she was supposed to get dressed in five minutes and still had to cook the chicken and make the guacamole and salsa, Maggie left the cakes cooling and got back to work. She peeled, chopped, minced, sliced, diced, mixed, stirred, and sautéed until her fingers were red from juggling utensils and tears trickled down her cheeks from onion fumes. At exactly 5:50, with the guacamole and salsa done and the chicken sizzling in the pan, she dashed to her room to get dressed.

She was glad she'd planned her outfit and laid it out ahead of time. It took her three minutes and six seconds to blow-dry the flour out of her hair and put on lip gloss and mascara, which left six minutes and fifty-four seconds to get dressed. By the time she stood in front of her full-length mirror, she still had an entire minute to inspect her appearance.

Maggie turned to the right and then the left for a complete view. Her hair and skin were flour-free. The purple skirt, white button-down shirt, and purple V-neck sweater looked great together, and the purple suede flats she'd bought just for the occasion were even cuter than she remembered.

There was just one thing missing.

"Perfect," she whispered, sliding on the silver bracelet with the aquamarine stone.

As she took one last look in the mirror, she felt good. She hadn't been sleeping much since getting her history report grade, but she felt more awake than she had in weeks. So she'd made mistakes, and let people down. So she was no longer a straight-A student. The romantics were right—love conquered all. It had gotten her parents through some very tough times that they might never have survived otherwise, and now they were happier than they'd ever been. And with Arnie by her side, it would get her through the eighth grade.

The doorbell rang at six o'clock sharp, and Maggie bolted out of her room and down the hallway. Her smile grew as she neared the door, and by the time she flung it open, she was trying not to giggle in nervous excitement.

"Arnie?" Her smile vanished. "What *happened*?"

"Hey, Maggie," he said, trying to grin and gasp for air at the same time. "Great scavenger hunt."

She looked from the red envelope he squeezed in one hand, to the bike he held upright with the other.

"Where's Dad Junior? Or Little Mom?" She peered around him to check the driveway. It was empty. "You rode your *bike* here? Your house is twenty minutes away by car."

"And you usually wear shoes in the car."

Maggie's eyes fell to his feet. "Slipper socks?"

"I told you they were awesome." He lifted up one foot proudly so she could see the argyle pattern.

She stepped onto the front stoop, took the bike from him and leaned it against the side of the house, and gently pulled him inside.

"DJ and LM had off today," Arnie explained, fanning his

face with the envelope. "And since the invitation you sent said to meet you at Java the Hut, which is right around the corner from my house, I figured slipper socks would be fine."

"But Java the Hut was just the first leg of—"

"Your ten-legged scavenger hunt," he finished. "I know that now."

"Oh, Arnie," Maggie said, shaking her head. "I'm so sorry. I had no idea you didn't have a ride."

"No worries." His breathing had slowed enough for him to grin. "How would you have known? And it was a great hunt. Really."

Maggie frowned. She *would've* known if she'd thought to ask before leaving notes and clues all over town.

"And it works out," he continued, "because now I'm starving. And your last hint said something about a fabulous feast . . . ?"

"Yes," she said, still feeling guilty but happy to move on. The rest of the night would definitely make up for its rough start. "And it *will* be fabulous."

"Let me guess—chicken?"

She elbowed him playfully as they started for the kitchen. "How'd you know?"

His face scrunched as he looked at her. "Because I think it might be burning."

He said this just as they reached the kitchen doorway—and Maggie heard the chicken still sizzling in the frying pan.

"*No,*" she groaned, flying to the stove and yanking the pan from the burner. The charred strips looked more like bacon than chicken. "I just wanted it to stay warm while I got dressed!"

"It's okay." Arnie joined her and casually turned the burner from high to off. "A feast always has more than one part, right?"

"Right." She stared at the chicken like it was just too hot and would regain its normal color once it cooled off. When it didn't, she turned to Arnie and forced a smile. "There are cheese, crackers, and water on the dining room table. Why don't you make yourself comfortable in there while I get everything else ready?"

"Will do." He patted her back. "Don't be long."

She didn't want to be long. She wanted to have dinner so that they could have dessert and keep things going from there . . . but first she had to figure out how to salvage the main course. Trying to stay calm, she scraped the burnt chicken into the trash, dropped the pan in the sink, and searched the refrigerator for backup.

"Vegetarian fajitas!" she declared ten minutes later, entering the dining room with a silver tray.

"I love fajitas!" Arnie sat at one end of the dining room table and raised his water glass. "See? Who needs chicken?"

She placed the tray on the table and pointed to the various bowls. "Whole-wheat tortillas, refried beans, low-fat cheddar cheese, green peppers and onions, and, the best parts—salsa and guacamole, made by hand, by yours truly."

Feeling like she'd just reached the finish line after running a marathon, Maggie dropped into the chair across from Arnie's and spread a red cloth napkin in her lap. She was glad she'd thought to set the table earlier.

"Are your parents eating too?"

"Nope. Not here, anyway." Maggie motioned for his plate and piled a little bit of everything onto it. She smiled sweetly as she handed it back to him. "We have the whole place to ourselves."

"Oh. Great." He took the plate and looked at it for a second before putting it down. "Do you always set extra places then? Just in case unexpected visitors stop by during dinner?"

Maggie giggled when she realized what he was talking about. Because she'd set the table while her parents were still home, she'd had to set it for four people instead of two. "I told my parents that Aimee and Peter were coming over."

"Are they?"

"No," Maggie said, puzzled. He'd almost sounded hopeful. "That was just what I said so you and I could hang out alone."

"Oh. Good idea."

Noticing the tall candles lining the middle of the table were still unlit, Maggie jumped up. As she did, her right knee struck the bottom of the tabletop, which made her water glass topple over and Arnie lunge for his to prevent the same outcome. She quickly mopped up the water with her napkin, and ran for the living room. After grabbing a box of matches from the coffee table, she swung by the stereo and popped in a CD, and then dashed back to the dining room.

"That's better," she said breathlessly, lighting the candles. "Much more romantic, don't you think?"

"Um . . . sure." He drained his water glass. "I didn't know you liked classical music."

"It's Mozart." She blew out the match and sat down. "My mom and dad sometimes dance to this song when they think Summer and I aren't paying attention."

Arnie nodded as he refilled his water glass.

"Don't you think that's great? That two people can still be so in love after so much time together? I think that's so great. Finding that kind of love has to be the most important thing in the whole world." She watched him drink another glass of water, and then a third. When he went to refill the glass again, she looked at his plate. "Arnie? Is something wrong with your dinner?"

"What?" He set the water pitcher down harder than he'd intended, and winced at sound of glass hitting wood. "No. Not at all. It's delicious." He grabbed his fork and lifted a mound of beans.

"Your food has moved *around* your plate . . . but it hasn't moved *from* your plate." She quickly assembled her own fajita and took a bite. It tasted fine. Not as good as it would've with chicken, but definitely edible.

They ate in silence for several minutes. Maggie didn't want to pay attention to what Arnie was doing with his food, but she couldn't help it. In the time it took her to finish two stuffed fajitas, he ate a small piece of tortilla sprinkled with shredded cheese. This probably would've been enough to send her into a full-fledged panic attack if dinner wasn't only one small part of her master plan. But since it was, she monitored the clock hanging on the wall behind Arnie; at 6:58, she started gathering dishes.

"Ready for dessert?" she asked.

"Yes," he said, like he thought she'd never ask.

She was relieved when the miniature chocolate cakes were

a huge success. With the exception of their sunken middles, which Maggie filled with whipped cream, they'd turned out just like the recipe said they would. She only had a taste, since Arnie devoured three immediately and she wanted him to have as much as he wanted, but it was enough to know that they were rich, moist, and delicious. The only way dessert could've gone better was if they'd actually talked and laughed while enjoying it.

But it was still an improvement, and Maggie was determined to take advantage of the upswing. At 7:29, she suggested they move into the living room—and then waited two more minutes as Arnie polished off the cakes.

"Don't tell the Patrol This kids," he joked, licking the chocolate from his fingers.

"I'll bring the candles," she said quickly. Along with the swim team and history class, Patrol This was the last thing she wanted to think about right then.

"Wow," Arnie said once they'd moved to the living room.

"Merry Christmas in September!" Immediately dismissing the dinner debacle, Maggie held out both arms like Arnie was on *The Price Is Right* and had just won the room's entire contents in the final showcase showdown.

Arnie's eyes landed on a mountain of presents sitting under the potted fern in the corner of the room. "Those are for *me*?"

"Yes." She hurried across the room and lifted as many brightly colored packages as her arms could hold. "But if my parents ask, you, Aimee, and Peter all loved the back-to-school rulers, protractors, and Number Two pencils I gave you."

"Maggie," Arnie said, sinking to the couch. "You didn't have to do this."

"I know I didn't have to," she said happily, sitting next to him. "But I really, really wanted to."

He looked at her and smiled, and for just a second, she thought it would happen right then. She thought he might be so touched by the gifts that he would lean over and plant a quick, grateful kiss on her lips.

"Open them," she said, just in case. Because it wasn't time yet.

He looked at the presents like he didn't think he should, but after a few seconds, his smile grew and he gave in. "Guitar Hero World Tour?" he exclaimed, tearing the wrapping paper from the first present and tossing it to the floor. "Maggie, this costs, like, fifty dollars."

"Do you have it?" she asked.

He stared at the cover and shook his head.

"Do you like it? Will it make you happy?"

Still staring at the cover, he nodded.

She grinned. "Then that's all that matters."

She had to remind him of this after the next present, and then next one, and the one after that. Three video games, four CDs, two DVDs, and one four-pack of Sugar-Free Red Bull later, she was still promising him that the money wasn't an issue.

"We do get paid for babysitting the little ones every week," she reminded him.

"Yeah, but not much." He leaned back on the couch and hugged his presents to his chest. "And you said you wanted to use that money to build your personal library and start saving toward college."

She shrugged. College was part of her future . . . but she hoped it wasn't the only part.

"Arnie," she said quickly after checking her watch and seeing that it was already 8:03—three minutes later than she'd planned to start the date's next phase. "I wanted to talk to you."

"I'm always here to listen." He flashed her a quick smile before picking up a DVD case and reading the back.

She slid closer to him on the couch and gently pressed down on the DVD case. "It's kind of important."

He looked at her. Seeing that she was serious, he lifted the presents from his chest, placed them on the coffee table, and shifted on the couch so he faced her. "What's wrong?"

"Nothing." She smiled. They sat so close now that his right knee touched her left one. "Everything's great, actually. Couldn't be better."

"Okay . . ."

She took a deep breath. This was it. The last step before the main event. She'd written out everything she wanted to say and read the small speech until it was memorized. She'd recited it in front of her bedroom mirror a dozen times, and even practiced accompanying facial expressions and hand gestures. In a way, this was the final test. And it was one she couldn't afford to fail.

"Arnie," she started, hoping her voice sounded more normal to him than it did to her, "I gave you these gifts because I thought they would make you happy."

"They do," he said when she paused for his response. "Thank you."

"You're welcome," she said, relieved when he answered the way she'd thought he would. "I wanted to make you happy, because that's what you do for me every single day."

"Well, that's—"

She held up one hand. "Please. Let me finish."

He raised his eyebrows and scooted back on the couch.

Her eyes shifted to his right knee, which was now several

inches from her left one. "Arnie, the thing is, I really like you." She lifted her eyes to his. "I really, *really* like you. More than I've ever liked anyone. When I have a bad day, thinking about you makes it better. When I'm stressed, hearing your voice makes me calmer. You're my first thought when I wake up, and my last one before I fall asleep."

She paused. During rehearsals, this was when she allotted five seconds for him to grab her hand and say, "Maggie, I feel the exact same way." But he didn't grab her hand. He didn't say anything. He simply stared at her without blinking.

She looked down at her purple suede flats as her cheeks warmed. "Anyway . . . I just wanted you to know all of this, because I wanted you to know that I'm ready. I'm ready to take our relationship to the next level. We were good friends, and we've been a good couple." She made herself look up. This was the last line, the clincher, the one after which nothing would be the same. "But I'm ready to be *great*."

The only light in the living room came from the candles on the coffee table. The soft sounds of violins and cellos surrounded them. The moment was as romantic as she'd planned it to be.

"Arnie . . . ," she whispered, leaning toward him and closing her eyes.

"Maggie."

Still leaning toward him, she opened her eyes. Arnie had leaned away from her, and was holding his stomach with both hands and sweating like he'd just ridden his bike up Mount Everest in slipper socks.

"I'm so sorry . . . ," he whispered. "But I think I'm going to be sick."

She couldn't move as he jumped up from the couch. By the time her legs realized her brain was screaming at them to run, he'd already darted from the living room and through the dining room. She reached the front door just in time to watch him pedal down the driveway and disappear up the road. After a few minutes, when he didn't return, she went inside and closed the door.

She stopped by the kitchen on her way back to the living room. And until nine o'clock sharp, when she heard her dad's car pull in the driveway, she sat on the couch listening to Mozart, watching the candles cast shadows around the room . . . and eating the chocolate bars leftover from her perfect dessert.

20. "Milky Ways, Snickers, Twix, and Three Musketeers."

Maggie opened her eyes to see a red whistle dangling above her nose.

"Not exactly a breakfast of champions, Bean."

"I'm not exactly a champion, Ms. P."

Maggie reached into her backpack pocket, grabbed a handful of M&M's, and dropped them in her mouth. "Besides, I already had chocolate chip pancakes with extra maple syrup for breakfast. This is my midmorning snack."

"It's seven o'clock."

"When you've been up since three, seven's midmorning." She closed her eyes and reached for another handful of M&M's.

"How'd you get in here, anyway? School doesn't start for half an hour."

Maggie pointed to the bag on the floor.

"Butterfingers?"

"The custodian's favorite." She dropped the M&M's into her mouth, one by one. "A few more bags of those and I'll have my own key to the principal's office."

Which would probably come in handy, considering her recent academic downward spiral. She'd never considered herself the breaking-and-entering, computer-hacking type, but maybe she should give it a try. She had nothing left to lose if she got in trouble, and if she got caught she'd probably get suspended . . . and she could definitely go for an extended vacation.

"Bean."

"Ms. P," Maggie sighed, "no offense, but I'm really not in the mood for a lecture."

Ms. Pinkerton paused. "I was just going to ask if you had any Kit Kats."

Maggie opened her eyes again. Ms. Pinkerton leaned over her, her normally scowling face a combination of embarrassed and hopeful. Maggie sat up slowly, the movement sending a flurry of candy wrappers from the diving board to the white tiles below, and lifted her backpack to her lap. She sifted through the plastic bags until she found the Kit Kats, and handed them to Ms. Pinkerton.

"Thank you," Ms. Pinkerton exhaled, taking the bag and sitting on the other end of the diving board. "And I know what you're thinking."

Maggie doubted that, considering all she could think since Arnie's abrupt departure two days before was that she'd never felt worse in her entire life. She felt worse than she did when she weighed 186 pounds. And when she couldn't finish the annual mile run in gym class. And when Anabel and Julia made fun of the black swimsuit with the waist ruffle she'd worn to try to hide her belly. And when her parents made her go to Pound Patrollers with Aunt Violetta. And when she didn't make the Water Wings. And even when she told Peter Applewood that she liked him as more than a friend, and he didn't feel the same way.

"Get a grip."

Maggie's head snapped toward Ms. Pinkerton. "Excuse me?"

"Get a grip." Ms. Pinkerton ripped open a Kit Kat packet and crammed two full wafers in her mouth. "That's what you're thinking. It's obvious by the silly skirts and high heels I've been forcing myself into every day that I don't need Kit Kats. I need to get a grip."

"I wasn't thinking that." Maggie peered over Ms. Pinkerton's shoulder to the sparkling pool water behind her. "In fact, I think you should have as many Kit Kats as you

Tricia Rayburn

want. You should have as many Kit Kats as it will take for you to feel better."

"The factory doesn't make that much in a year."

Maggie looked at the dozens of candy wrappers littering the tiled floor. She knew how Ms. Pinkerton felt.

"Anyway, Bean, I don't know *why* you're here, but I'm glad you're here. And not just because of the free chocolate."

"Then why?" Maggie asked, unable to come up with another reason, since Ms. Pinkerton never seemed glad to see any of her students. And it wasn't like Maggie was especially good company these days.

Ms. Pinkerton finished one Kit Kat and immediately opened another. "Do you know that, up until a few days ago, I hadn't cried in thirty-four years?"

Maggie's chin dropped. That was almost three times as long as Maggie'd been alive—and Maggie had probably cried hundreds of times since being born. "Not once?"

"Nope."

"Not at movies? Or to get out of a speeding ticket? Or when you broke an arm, or a leg, or whatever?"

Ms. Pinkerton shook her head. "The last time I cried was when my childhood dog, Squat, died."

Maggie watched Ms. Pinkerton shove another wafer in her mouth. "You named your childhood dog Squat?"

Ms. Pinkerton's eyes flicked to Maggie's and narrowed. "I'm trying to have a moment here, Bean. Want to guess how often I do that?"

"Never." It wasn't a guess.

"Anyway, every minute that I wasn't at school Squat and I spent together. When I went to the fishing hole, he carried my rod in his mouth. When I watched TV, he rested his head on my lap. When I went to bed, he curled up at my feet and stayed there all night."

"He sounds like a good dog," Maggie said, trying—and failing—to picture a young Ms. Pinkerton hanging out at a fishing hole.

"He *was* a good dog. He was the best dog." Ms. Pinkerton sighed. "And when he was gone, I thought my life was over. Because I'd never known life without him, and I didn't know what to do when he wasn't there anymore."

Maggie nodded and looked down. She knew how that felt too. She hadn't heard from Arnie after their disastrous romantic evening, and she'd been having trouble filling the hours since then. Which was why she'd been sleeping and gorging on chocolate. If she was asleep, she couldn't think about how she'd ruined everything, and sugar comas were basically like sleeping with your eyes open. They weren't exactly productive activities, but they passed the time.

"I cried for days," Ms. Pinkerton said. "For weeks. I couldn't sleep. I couldn't eat. I couldn't do anything but think of all the fun we had that we would never have again. And later—much, *much* later—I vowed that I would never let myself feel that kind of pain again. It was just too hard."

"I'm sorry," Maggie said after a minute.

"It was the toughest thing I'd ever gone through. And because of my vow, it *remained* the toughest thing I had to go through—until this summer."

Maggie looked down at her sneakers, remembering what Julia had said about Ms. Pinkerton's relationship during the first gym class of the year.

"I don't like to talk about my personal life, Bean—to anyone, let alone my students. But I'm telling you this now because I think you deserve an explanation for my recent behavior. I trust that whatever I say will stay between us. Are we clear?"

"Crystal," Maggie promised, even though part of her wanted to hide in the locker room, or dive into the pool and wait underwater until Ms. Pinkerton went to her office. She didn't know if she'd ever want to hear details about Ms. Pinkerton's love life, but it felt especially strange now, when her own love life had suffered such an early, tragic death.

"Ten years ago, I met Junior in the produce aisle of the supermarket. We both grabbed the last honeydew melon at the same time, and proceeded to argue for fifteen minutes about who should get to leave the store with it."

"I bet you won that argument," Maggie said.

"No bets about it, Bean." Ms. Pinkerton tore open another Kit Kat. "The following week, we ran into each other at the deli counter and argued over whether ham or turkey was the better cold cut. The week after that, we met in the freezer aisle and debated the nutritional value of frozen spinach versus fresh spinach. The week after that, we met in the dairy aisle and he asked me out to dinner. When I said no, he opened a carton of eggs and juggled six at once." She looked at Maggie. "Have you ever seen anyone do that?"

Maggie shook her head.

"Trust me—it's impressive. He didn't drop one. Not *one*."

"Wow."

"You said it. I was a goner after that. We were together for ten years."

Maggie waited as Ms. Pinkerton chewed and swallowed another chocolate wafer.

"He wanted to get married right away, but I wasn't ready. He proposed every year for nine years . . . and I turned him down every single time."

"Why?" Maggie asked. "If you were that crazy about him and knew you wanted to be with him, why not make it official?"

Ms. Pinkerton shrugged. "I was nervous. I thought if we got married, things would change. And they were already so good the way they were."

Maggie nodded. She didn't know if she'd be able to say no to someone she loved so many times, but she understood not wanting to mess up a good thing—especially now.

"But *last* year . . . ," Ms. Pinkerton continued. "Last year, I was ready. Every time we went on a date, I hoped that night would be the night that he asked the question again. I wanted to say yes more than anything. I finally wanted to take the plunge—I wanted to get married and live happily ever after."

"So what happened?" Maggie asked gently.

"There was no proposal—at least not from him."

"*You* proposed?"

"I did. On the last day of school last year, I called him from work and asked him to stop by the supermarket and pick up a honeydew melon for dessert later that night. When he got to the produce aisle, I was waiting for him. On one knee."

"Ms. P!" Maggie exclaimed, temporarily forgetting her own heartbreak. "That's so sweet!"

"*Thank* you." Ms. Pinkerton slapped her knee, like she was happy someone had finally appreciated the gesture. "That's what I thought. Unfortunately, Junior didn't agree. Or if he did, it wasn't enough for him to say yes."

"Oh." Maggie grabbed two full-size Snickers from her backpack and handed one to Ms. Pinkerton.

"Yeah. And then right after that, he said he needed space. He needed time to think." She ripped off the Snickers wrapper, took a big bite, and looked at Maggie. "He's still thinking."

"That's ridiculous," Maggie said automatically. "What's there to think about? He's been waiting for you to be ready, and you're ready. Bring on the wedding bells."

"Yes, well . . . while he's been thinking, I've been trying to become someone else. Someone completely different from me, since he obviously didn't want *me*." She looked down at her brown suede pants and sparkly orange heels. "And I've been trying really hard not to worry about it, but I am. I've been a mess. It's been like losing Squat all over again."

Maggie frowned and took another bite of her Snickers bar.

"Anyway, Bean, that's why I broke down in front of you last week. When you told me the swim team was done, I realized how obsessing about Junior was taking me away from my other responsibilities. So when I cried for the first time in thirty-four years, it wasn't just because I miss Junior. It was because I was so upset for neglecting you and the rest of the swim team. I mean, I let those crazy Water Wings just float in and fill an entire period with preposterous propaganda!"

"Yes," Maggie said with a nod. "Yes, you did."

"It wasn't fair, Bean. I lost my head. And I apologize."

"It's okay, Ms. P. Really. Like I said, it was pretty much a lost cause to begin with."

Ms. Pinkerton started to say something but stopped when the locker room doors on the other side of the pool flew open.

"Carla?" Maggie called out, squinting to make out the petite sixth grader's face.

"Oh, hey, Maggie!" Carla yelled back. "Sorry, I didn't realize anyone was here. I usually have the pool to myself until the first bell. But that's okay! I'll just come back later, or tomorrow, or whenever it's convenient for you."

Maggie suddenly noticed Carla was wearing a yellow swimsuit and blue goggles. "You swim here?"

"Every morning, now that I'm not meeting you and Aimee at the petition table."

"How do you get in?"

"Easy." Carla shrugged. "Buster the custodian will do anything for a few Butterfingers."

Maggie's chin dropped. Not only did Carla know how to win over the custodian, she knew his name. Maggie hadn't known his name until Carla said it, and she'd been going to the school two years longer.

"Anyway, sorry to interrupt! I'll just—"

"It's okay," Maggie said. "Stay. Swim."

As Carla ran for the pool and dove in, Maggie and Ms. Pinkerton started gathering the candy wrappers from the diving board and tile floor. Ms. Pinkerton talked about the factual inaccuracies of Mrs. Swanson's and Mrs. Richards's special presentation, but Maggie hardly heard her. She was too busy watching Carla. Carla was little, but she was strong—and fast. Her arms and legs sliced through the water like it was air, and each time she reached a wall, she somersaulted and kept going without slowing down.

"Ms. P," Maggie said once her backpack was stuffed with empty wrappers. She nodded toward Carla. "How does she do that?"

"You mean zip through the water like a torpedo?" Ms. Pinkerton shrugged. "She's tiny. Tiny people move faster than those who eat Kit Kats for their midmorning snacks."

"Not that," Maggie said. "I meant . . . how is she smiling? Without drowning?"

Carla was doing the crawl and dipping her face in the

water with every other stroke. Each time she lifted her face out of the water, her smile lit up the natatorium brighter than the afternoon sun. Maggie had never seen anything like it, and didn't know how it was physically possible.

"I don't know," Ms. Pinkerton said after a minute. "I guess when you're doing what you love, you just find a way."

Maggie considered this. She remembered the very first time she went swimming in the school pool. She'd never felt so light and so strong at the same time. After that it didn't matter how she felt *out* of the pool so long as she was able to get *in* the pool every day. Was that how Carla felt now? Was that how she would've felt every day for the next three years, if they'd been able to save the swim team?

"Ms. P . . . the school board meeting isn't for four more days."

Ms. Pinkerton looked at Maggie, surprised. When Maggie didn't say anything else, Ms. Pinkerton nodded and crossed her arms over her chest.

"Don't worry, Bean. We'll find a way."

21. "Just remember, Mags. Whatever's meant to be, will be."

"Oh?" Maggie raised her eyebrows at Aimee as they hurried toward the auditorium. "What happened to taking down the breath-holding bloodsuckers? And breaking the circle of floating floozies?"

"Yoga happened. Last week I told my parents that I would make the decision they wanted me to as long as they did something for *me*. When I said that that something was for them to stop fighting all the time, Mom signed us up for a yoga class so that we could work toward inner—and outer—peace. I think she did that so we wouldn't have to actually *talk* about anything, but so far, it seems to be working."

"Wow."

Aimee glanced over her shoulder to her parents following close behind. "I can't remember the last time they stood so close to each other without yelling."

"That's great," Maggie said. "And it was nice of them to come today."

"Yes, well, as soon as I announced this morning that I wanted to live with Mom, Dad whipped out a calendar and started coordinating our schedules. I'll probably see them both more now than I did before."

"And you're doing okay?" Maggie asked. "Feeling good about your decision?"

"I am. I'm sure we'll have our moments, but, like I said— whatever's meant to be will be." When they reached the auditorium door, Aimee leaned toward Maggie and lowered her voice. "But truthfully? I *do* hope we take down the float-ing floozies. A thousand hours in the downward-facing-dog position won't change that."

Maggie grinned, took a deep breath, and pushed open the auditorium door.

"Welcome from the Water Wings!"

Maggie and Aimee froze in the doorway when Mrs. Richards and Mrs. Swanson thrust silver goodie bags at them. Maggie could see more iTunes gift cards, a Starbucks gift card, and an iPod arm band poking through the curly silver ribbons wrapped around the bags' handles.

"Inner peace," Aimee whispered as they pushed between the mothers without taking the bags. "Inner peace. Inner peace. Inner—"

"Over here, Bean!"

Maggie followed the booming voice across the auditorium until she spotted Ms. Pinkerton standing on a chair and waving both arms in the air. The chairs around hers were filled with other swim team members and their families and friends. It was an impressive turnout, but any happiness Maggie felt at the show of support disappeared once she took in the rest of the room.

The auditorium's seating was divided into three sections. Two sections, each ten seats wide, ran along the far walls. The swim team crowd filled half of one of those sections.

The middle section, which took up most of the room, was thirty seats wide. Silver streamers ran down the aisles, and big bunches of silver balloons were attached by silver ribbons to the end chairs of every row. And there wasn't one empty seat, as the Water Wings and their supporters filled the entire section.

"It's like a wedding," Aimee said.

"After the champagne's gone," Maggie added. The Water Wings fans were already cheering and yelling like rowdy guests at a wedding reception.

The noise only grew louder as they made their way further into the auditorium. By the time they reached the swim team section, Maggie's ears were ringing and she was wishing she'd joined Aimee's family's yoga class too. She didn't think it was possible to feel *peaceful* while surrounded by the cacophony of cheers and whistles, but maybe she wouldn't have wanted to wage war quite as much.

"Here's the plan, Bean," Ms. Pinkerton barked once Maggie and Aimee were within earshot. "We drew straws to see who would go first, and they won."

"*They're* going first?" Maggie groaned. "We'll never be able to get people's attention after they've given out free cars, trips around the world, and whatever else they have planned."

"Don't panic, Bean. It's better this way. They're just the opening act to our main event, the appetizer to our entrée."

Maggie started to respond, but stopped when she noticed Ms. Pinkerton's baggy gym shorts, T-shirt, and sneakers. She looked like her old self again.

"So after they get the crowd warmed up for us, I'll say my spiel, and then the floor's yours." Ms. Pinkerton winked at Maggie. "We're almost there."

As Maggie looked around the room, she thought that that much was true. Regardless of the outcome, in another hour, the fight would be over. And the next day, she'd be staying after school for practice . . . or going home, staring at the phone, and willing it to ring.

"Is he here?"

Maggie scanned the auditorium once more before dropping into the chair next to Aimee's. "Nope."

"You really haven't talked since the big date?"

"You mean the ginormous disaster?" Maggie sighed. "No, we haven't. He hasn't called, and neither have I."

"Mags, if you want something, you have to do everything you can to get it. That's why we're here right now, isn't it?"

"Aim, I *did* do everything I could. That was the problem. What I wanted obviously wasn't what he wanted, and now we're not even talking, which was the *last* thing I wanted."

"We'll fix it, don't worry." Aimee squeezed Maggie's hand. "But for now, let's stay focused. Are you ready? Do you want to go over anything?"

Maggie was about to suggest crawling under the chair and staying there until the meeting was over when the auditorium lights suddenly went out.

"Perfect," Maggie whispered as the room fell silent. "If the electricity's out, maybe they'll postpone the decision and we can have a few more days to prepare."

Before Aimee could answer, the auditorium filled with

a sound that resembled a hundred delicate wind chimes singing in the breeze. The sound started out soft as it surrounded them, but quickly grew louder. A spotlight shot out from somewhere near the ceiling just as a glittering disco ball lowered from the rafters over the stage. The ball spun faster as the chimes rang louder, causing the entire auditorium to sparkle like a swirling snow globe. Maggie closed her eyes when she started to feel dizzy, but immediately opened them again when the chimes and disco ball were replaced by techno music and strobe lights.

"Inner peace!" Aimee shouted over the noise as a pair of silver wings shone against a stage-to-ceiling screen hanging at the back of the stage.

"I can't feel my feet!" Maggie shouted back. It was true. The music was so loud, the floor was vibrating and making her feet numb.

The Water Wings opening act, which was a cross between a music video, a dance club, and a pep rally, lasted fifteen minutes. The music dulled only once, when the school's cheerleaders ran onstage to get everyone on their feet and chanting along to, "When I say 'Water,' you say 'Wings,'" and "We love the Wings, they give us things." The cheerleaders were followed by members of the football, soccer, tennis, and track teams, who ran across the stage in uniform and tossed Water Wings paraphernalia into the crowd. As they tossed, a pair of silver sunglasses hit Aimee in the head, and a silver beach towel emblazoned with a pair of wings landed in Maggie's lap. At the end of the performance, the entire middle section screamed and stomped as the Water Wings team walked onstage in their silver swimsuits. They formed a perfectly straight line that stretched from one end of the stage to the other, looped their arms around each other's waists, and bowed.

"That's it?" Aimee yelled when the auditorium lights came back on.

"Isn't that enough?" Maggie yelled back.

"But they didn't *say* anything," Aimee insisted. "The board doesn't care about free stuff. We still have a chance!"

Maggie looked to the board members, who sat at a long table at one end of the stage, banging gavels and speaking into microphones to get the crowd's attention. After almost ten minutes, when people finally stopped screaming and started sitting down, Principal Marshall took center stage.

"Thank you," he said loudly into a microphone. "Thank you, Water Wings, for that, um, interesting performance. And thank you to everyone for coming out in support of your classmates. We're very happy to see such enthusiasm, and regret that it's prompted by such unfortunate circumstances. That said, I'd like to invite representatives from the swim team onstage for their rebuttal."

Trying not to dwell on the fact that their introduction came right after a reference to unfortunate circumstances, Maggie took the clipboard and notebook Aimee handed her, and followed Ms. Pinkerton to the stage. She waited on the stage steps as Ms. Pinkerton greeted the board and presented them with a variety of swim team accomplishments and statistics. Maggie didn't think anyone in the middle section heard one word, but Ms. Pinkerton still spoke confidently, and the board definitely listened.

As Ms. Pinkerton gave her closing remarks, Maggie scanned the crowd once more. She was nervous—more nervous than she'd been since trying out for the Water Wings almost a year before—and she hoped for the one familiar face that would help keep her calm. Arnie had been in the bleachers during those tryouts. He'd cheered her on while holding a big sign that he'd made himself with glue and glitter.

But that was then, and this was now. She hadn't talked to Arnie in almost a week to tell him about the meeting, and even if she had, she doubted he would've come.

Her eyes landed on Aimee, and her heart lifted briefly when Aimee waved and pointed behind her. Maggie smiled as she spotted her mom, dad, and Summer sitting a few rows back, sharing a bag of popcorn like the meeting was a movie. Since Maggie had driven there with Aimee, she didn't know when her parents would arrive, or where they would sit when they did. They weren't who she was really hoping to see, but she was still glad they were there.

When it was her turn to speak, she jogged up the rest of the steps. Her cheeks burned and her heart thudded in her ears as she hurried across the stage. She was grateful to hear the swim team section cheering and clapping, but was aware that the middle section was completely quiet.

"You can do it, Bean," Ms. Pinkerton whispered before turning the microphone over to Maggie.

"Hi." Maggie tried to smile at the crowd, and then looked down. The spotlight was so bright she couldn't see anything or anyone. "Um, like Mr. Marshall said, thank you for coming out in support of us. It really means a lot. And Mr. Marshall, thank you and the board for giving us this chance to fight for our teams."

Mr. Marshall nodded and the rest of the board smiled politely.

"So . . ." She squinted against the light as she forced herself to look back out at the auditorium. "As many of you have heard by now, the swim team does wonderful things for its members. It promotes physical activity and personal health. It encourages friendly competition. It fosters camaraderie and a sense of community. And perhaps most importantly, it helps young women feel more confident."

"We've heard it all before!"

Maggie swallowed as the male voice called out from somewhere in the middle. His outburst caused whispers and giggle to ripple throughout the room.

"You *have* heard it all before," Maggie continued, tightening her hold on the notebook and clipboard as her palms grew moist. "That's because for several weeks, we've been doing our best to educate the school community about the benefits of the swim team. We appreciate your listening, and are happy so many of you signed our petition to show your support."

"Excuse me, Mr. Marshall!"

The clipboard slipped from Maggie's hand and clattered to the stage as Anabel Richards jumped up from her chair.

"Miss Richards, I'm sure Miss Bean will be happy to answer any questions you may have as soon as she's done speaking."

"But it's *important*, Mr. Marshall."

Maggie caught Ms. Pinkerton's eye as Anabel ran onstage.

"Thanks so much, Maggie," Anabel cooed as she took the microphone in one hand and nudged Maggie aside. "This will just take a second."

Maggie wanted to grab the microphone back, but knew that at this point, coming across as the saner, more mature organization was probably the only thing they had going for them. So she stepped back without protest.

"The Water Wings and I would just like to make sure the board knows that we *also* educated the school community and started a petition." She held up the rhinestone-encrusted clipboard for all to see. "We were so touched by the outpouring of support. I mean, we expected a lot of signatures—but in the end, *four hundred and fifty-three* of our wonderful classmates signed our petition. And we thank them. We thank them all!"

Maggie tried to smile as Anabel blew kisses to the audience, curtsied, and presented their petition to the board, but she couldn't move her lips.

The Water Wings had gotten 453 signatures. Even after Maggie, Aimee, and several of the swim team members had blanketed the school over the past four days, they'd only boosted their count to 185.

She was so stunned, it took her several seconds to realize that Anabel was back in her seat, and that everyone waited for her to continue. She was glad when Ms. Pinkerton gently pushed her forward, and her feet made it back to the microphone.

"Um . . . so, like I was saying—"

"Yeah, *what* was that again?" another male voice called out.

"I don't think you've really said anything yet!" a third shouted.

Maggie looked out at the crowd as a fresh wave of whispers and giggles started. Her eyes flicked back and forth, from the swim team section, to the middle section, and back. The spotlight suddenly felt like it was a thousand degrees, and she wished she could make out Aimee, or her parents, or Summer. If she could just spot an ally, one person in her corner who would smile at her and silently promise that everything was okay, she could get through it. She might not save the swim team, but she'd at least finish her presentation and make it out of the meeting without melting into a puddle onstage.

And then she saw it. At first she thought her fear and embarrassment were making her imagine things, but when she stepped away from the microphone and toward the edge of the stage, it was still there.

At the back of the room was a small blue cardboard sign

with glittery block letters that spelled out "Smile, BEANie Baby! This one's yours!"

It was the same sign Arnie had held up in the stands during Water Wings tryouts.

Her eyes had started to adjust as soon as she'd stepped out of the spotlight and toward the front of the stage. She could now see enough to make out individual faces in the crowd, and smiled as soon as she saw Arnie's peeking out from behind the sign. That was all she needed.

"You want to hear something you haven't heard before?" Maggie asked after darting back to the microphone. "A year ago, I decided to try out for the Water Wings. I decided this even though I weighed a hundred and eighty-six pounds that I tried to hide by wearing a swimsuit with a skirt."

"Maggie," Ms. Pinkerton whispered behind her as the crowd erupted in gasps and giggles. "This isn't what we talked about. You don't have to—"

"It's okay," Maggie promised. Her smile grew as she turned back to the audience. "I wanted to try out for the Water Wings for several reasons. At the time, I thought the most important ones were to look cute in the silver uniform, have an amazing circle of friends, and become instantly popular. And I did everything I could to make it happen. I even dieted and exercised until I passed out."

More gasps and giggles filled the room.

"Anyway, long story short, I didn't make the team." She looked down to Anabel and Julia, who pouted in the front row. "It doesn't matter why, but let's just say it wasn't because I forgot the routines. What *does* matter, is that I figured out what should've been the most important reason for trying out all along. And that was that in the water, I felt great. I felt strong, and healthy, and confident."

The gasps and giggles had faded, and now everyone listened attentively.

"After I joined the swim team, those feelings grew more every day. I didn't care what I looked like in the swimsuit, or how many new friends I made, or how popular I was. I just cared about swimming. And when that happened, when I focused only on how good it felt to be in the water, the rest followed." Maggie turned to the board. "I'm not saying that the Water Wings doesn't have its own benefits. But I *am* saying that their benefits aren't more—or better."

The board members exchanged looks as Maggie approached them.

"We only got a hundred and eighty-five signatures," she said, handing Mr. Marshall the clipboard. "But I know that over time, thousands of girls would love the chance to feel what I feel every time I'm in the pool."

"Well, of *course* you felt better when you joined the swim team!" a female voice shouted suddenly. "You weighed more than all the other members combined!"

Maggie's head snapped toward the crowd. She started for the edge of the stage for a better view of who'd just spoken, but stopped when a miniature torpedo came flying up the steps.

"Carla?"

"Hey, Maggie," Carla said, running up to her. "I think I can help. Do you mind if I try?"

Maggie paused, and then nodded. There was no way she could say no to her biggest fan now.

"My name's Carla Cooper." Carla stood on tiptoe to reach the microphone. "Most of you don't know me, because most of you don't have time for sixth graders. And that's fine—I know you're busy. But the thing is, most of you probably also don't have time for short people, or fat people, or people who read comic books, or who push their cars to school instead of drive them, and who keep their Christmas trees up all year long. Most of you don't really want to get to know people who, at first glance, seem kind of strange. And by strange, I mean different from you."

Maggie raised her eyebrows at Ms. Pinkerton, who nodded appreciatively.

"Anyway, that's why I swim—and I weigh ninety-three pounds, by the way. I swim because when I'm in the water, I don't feel small, or different. I just feel like me." She paused by the microphone, as if to give her words a chance to sink in. After a few seconds, she pulled a packet of papers from her pocket and dashed toward the board members. "That's two hundred and eleven more signatures for the swim team, courtesy of the sixth grade. Oh, and five more at the bottom, courtesy of the school custodial staff."

"Carla!" Maggie put one arm around her shoulders and squeezed. "That's amazing!"

"And here's a hundred and seven more, courtesy of the seventh- and eighth-grade guys."

Maggie's chin dropped as Peter Applewood hurried on stage and presented another packet of papers to the board.

"I waited at our lockers every day to talk to you about it," he said, offering her a small smile. "When that didn't work, I decided to try, anyway."

"Peter, *thank you*," Maggie said, suddenly feeling extremely silly for avoiding her locker. "I'm so sorry I've been MIA, I've just—"

"Mr. Marshall, esteemed board members, I'd like to say something, if that's okay."

"*Dad?*" Still thrown by Peter's presence next to her,

Maggie watched her dad lick popcorn butter from his fingers as he jogged up the steps.

"Hey, Mag Pie." Her dad gave her a quick wink and then turned to the board. "I wanted to discuss this with my daughter beforehand, but I just got approval this afternoon and didn't get to see her before the meeting."

"Approval for what?" Maggie eyed the envelope in his hand.

"For this." Her dad opened the envelope and took out a check. "Mr. Marshall, I'm a senior project manager for Ocean Vista Pools. Ocean Vista is very committed to giving back to the community, and would be honored to contribute to any maintenance and operating costs associated with the school pool. And by contribute, I mean cover."

"What?"

"Sorry, sweetie," her dad said, kissing the top of her head. "I wanted to tell you, but didn't want to get your hopes up if it didn't happen. I hope you don't mind."

Mind? Was he kidding?

"Mr. Bean, this is certainly very generous," Mr. Marshall said. "If you're sure, and if Ocean Vista's sure—"

"We are."

"Well," Mr. Marshall said, exchanging quick looks with the other board members. "We'll have to discuss the details . . . but if that's the case, I don't see why both teams can't continue."

As the adults shook hands and Ms. Pinkerton embraced a short man who'd jumped onstage and run right into her arms, Maggie looked out to the crowd.

Later, when she tried to recall everything about this moment, she might picture Anabel and Julia pouting at their mothers, Aimee hugging her parents, or the rest of the swim team exchanging high fives. She might hear the cheering and laughing, and feel the spotlight's heat still warm on her skin. But she knew that whenever she thought of this moment, she would always think of one thing first.

And that was the red cardboard sign with glittery block letters that spelled out **"I'M READY TO BE GREAT TOO."**

22.

"I think I'm tone-deaf," Maggie said when the TV squawked at her for the fifth time in five seconds.

"You're not tone-deaf. You're just dexterously challenged."

Maggie giggled, which made her fall even further behind. Her fingers scrambled up and down the plastic guitar neck as red, yellow, and blue notes flew toward the top of the TV screen.

"I think I see someone clapping." Arnie pointed to the animated audience when they booed Maggie's character offstage without letting her finish the song. "That guy there. He's totally buying your next record."

Maggie was laughing so hard tears filled her eyes. "Now I understand why so many rock stars freak out and start breaking instruments," she said, taking off the guitar. "It's not as easy as it looks."

"And all this time you thought I was just playing silly games," Arnie teased. "Guitar Hero is actually a challenging exercise designed to test and train your agility, hand-eye coordination—and patience."

"You must be *really* patient by now," Maggie said, wiping her eyes. "You could probably sit on a polar ice cap and wait for it to melt before standing up again."

"Probably," Arnie agreed with a grin. "Speaking of ice, would you like some with water? I'm going to grab a bottle from the kitchen."

"Sure. Thanks."

As Arnie headed for the kitchen, Maggie flopped on the couch. This was the first time they'd hung out since the last time, when Arnie had fled her house like it was on fire. And unlike that time, they hadn't planned to hang out. Maggie had been playing a late-morning game of Scrabble with her family when Arnie called and asked if she'd like to get together later in the day. She'd said yes without hesitating—or checking her schedule. She hadn't known what to expect when she got to his house, but was happy when there turned out to be no expectations. Arnie hadn't planned any specific activities, so they'd just been hanging out, talking, and laughing. And so far, it wasn't weird, or uncomfortable. In fact, it was probably the most fun they'd had together in weeks.

"So what do you want to do now?" Arnie asked, coming back into the room. He handed her a glass of water with ice, flopped on the couch, and rested his feet on the coffee table.

"I don't know." Maggie shrugged and put her feet on the table next to his. "What do *you* want to do now?"

"I don't know." He tapped her right foot with his left one. "I guess it depends on the rest of your day. Do you have a lot of homework? Or swim team practice? Or plans to meet up with Aimee?"

"Nope, nope, and nope. The only thing I have to do today is *not* have anything to do."

"That sounds like your best plan yet."

Maggie gently swirled the ice in her glass. She didn't want to ruin the casual, easygoing nature of their day, but there was one thing that needed to be talked about. And unfortunately, it couldn't wait.

"Arnie," she said.

"Maggie," he said at the same time.

They looked at each other and smiled.

"Is it okay if I go first?" he asked. "It's kind of important."

"Go ahead." Her heart raced as she wondered what important issue he wanted to talk about. Did he want to tell her everything that had bothered him over the past few weeks? Like how she hardly spoke on the corn maze date? And how she didn't seem to like the blueberry crepes as much as she should've at the country club party? And how he'd become the third wheel on their Bananarama date? And how she'd arranged a scavenger hunt without making sure he had adequate transportation first?

"I'm sorry."

"What?" She'd just taken a sip of water and had to force it down her throat. "*You're* sorry? Why?"

"Because I've never done this before." He looked at her, and then at the glass in his hands. "I've never been some-one's . . . boyfriend."

"Arnie," she said quickly, "you're the *best* boyfriend a girl could have. You could give classes on being sweet, and kind, and caring, and—"

"Pushy?" he added. "And scared?"

She frowned. If he'd been pushy and scared, she really hadn't been paying attention.

"Maggie, meeting you and becoming your friend was the best thing that'd ever happened to me. And then when I told you I liked you, and you felt the same way, *that* was the best thing that'd ever happened to me. So when we started going on dates, I think I kind of went a little crazy trying to make them perfect. I thought if I didn't, you might change your mind."

"Change my mind?"

"About me. About us. I thought if being more than friends wasn't what we both thought it should be, that we would go back to the way we were." He sighed. "That's why I planned the elaborate corn maze picnic. That's why I invited you to my parents' country club party without giving you more than an hour's notice."

"But an hour was all you had," Maggie protested. "That was when you found out about the extra tickets."

"Yes, but I didn't stop to think that it might not be fair to you, and of your time. All I could think was that there was this perfect, romantic night, already arranged, and that I had to do everything I could to get you there. And then when you were there, I was so nervous, I pigged out on blueberry crepes and poured powdered sugar on your dress."

"The crepes were delicious," she assured him. "And I had a great time."

He looked at her. "Do you know I've gained eight pounds since we started going out? Eight pounds of crepes, caramel apples, chocolate cake, and the cookies and chips I've been eating at home whenever I think I'm doing the wrong thing, or not doing enough."

"Oh, Arnie. I'm so sorry." She shook her head, instantly feeling terrible.

"It's okay—it's my fault. And it's nothing a few more Abdominator moves won't fix." He lifted his feet from the coffee table, sat up, and faced her. "The point is, Maggie . . . I was so worried about us going back to the way we were that I forgot how great that was. I was trying to change something that didn't need changing."

"I did the same thing," she said, her cheeks warming. "I thought being together meant that we were supposed to reach new levels—even though I didn't really know what those were, or how we got there. I became so worried about certain things happening at certain times, that I forgot to just enjoy the moment. That's why I planned that romantic dinner. I thought if I just cooked the right things, and picked the right music, and lit enough candles, that we'd become this amazing couple."

"And we already *were* an amazing couple."

She smiled.

"I'm sorry for that night too, by the way. You went to so much trouble, and I was too afraid of messing it up to not finish the scavenger hunt and ride my bike twenty miles in slipper socks." He paused. "I also couldn't admit that I'm allergic to tomatoes and avocadoes . . . and that beans give me migraines."

"Migraines?" Maggie groaned and clapped one hand to her forehead. "How did I not know that? I'm a terrible girlfriend. Break up with me now."

He looked at her, eyes wide. "That was a joke, right?"

"Yes," she said. "But as your girlfriend, I should probably know things like the foods that cause you pain."

"In that case, we should probably give the sweets a rest. Your chocolate cake was amazing, but I ate so much of it that my stomach held a grudge for days."

"Done."

He leaned back and put one arm around her shoulders. "So how about from now on, we plan to not plan quite so much? We'll just take each day one at a time, and go from there?"

"That sounds great," Maggie said, gently sliding out from under his arm and turning toward him. "I'm actually trying to plan less, in general. That's kind of what I wanted to talk to you about."

He looked confused. "But don't you love to plan? And juggle spreadsheets?"

"I don't know if 'love' is the right word. I was just so

determined to be the best student, daughter, friend, and girlfriend—especially after falling off the planet last summer—that I wanted to make sure nothing fell through the cracks."

"That's because you're you. You're responsible."

"I *tried* to be responsible," she corrected. "But it backfired. I was so busy, things started slipping. The mailing I messed up?"

"That was an accident." He shrugged. "They happen all the time."

"Not to me." She sighed. "Anyway, it got so bad that I gave up on the swim team. I convinced myself that it was okay that the Water Wings were winning the fight, because I was very busy and no longer needed the team the way I used to."

"Well, now you don't have to worry about that. The swim team was saved."

She nodded and lowered her eyes.

"Maggie." He leaned toward her. "What is it?"

"Too much." She looked at him. "It's too much. I wish I could do it all, but I can't. Not if I want to do what I do the right way."

He took her hand. "I'll fully support you if you decide to study less and play Guitar Hero more."

She laughed. "Unfortunately, I can't give up on the grades. I'm kind of biologically programmed for academic overachievement."

"But something has to go?" he asked gently.

"I have to study," she said. "I have to swim. I have to—because I want to—spend time with my family, Aimee, and you. Those things aren't negotiable."

"What does that leave? You can't really stop sleeping, eating, and showering."

She winced apologetically. "How effective do you think Electra's index card system is?"

"Patrol This?" He squeezed her hand. "Really?"

"I'll finish this session," she said quickly, "but after that . . . I think I might have to retire. I love the kids, and I love what we do, but it's a big commitment. I thought I could make it work with everything else, but I can't. And as much as I love it, at this point, it can't be my main priority."

He looked down at their clasped hands as he processed this. "Well," he said after a minute, "we'll all miss you. But maybe you can still contribute."

"Contribute?" she said doubtfully. She hated disappointing him, but when she moved on from the group, she thought it had to be a clean break.

"Yes." He raised his eyes to her and grinned. "Like,

maybe you can find a few minutes every now and then to review my new Abdominator workouts before I post them on the Web?"

She nodded thoughtfully. "I think that can probably be arranged."

"Great!" He jumped up, and still holding her hand, gently pulled her up with him. "I had an idea for the next one. I think it could be the best yet."

"Yeah? I'm all ears."

"Have you noticed how skinny all those rock stars are?" he asked, putting his arms around her waist and bringing her closer.

"They're twigs," she agreed. "Rails. Broom handles."

"Except for Meatloaf," he added. "Which is to be expected, I guess."

She grinned and looked up at him. "You're planning a Guitar Hero exercise?"

"We could call it 'Rock Out Workout.' What do you think?"

She wanted to answer, but was suddenly distracted by his voice growing softer, and his face nearing hers, and his eyes closing, and . . .

. . . their lips gently pressing together.

"I think," she whispered without opening her eyes once

his mouth lifted from hers, "that it's the best one yet."

As he hugged her tightly, she rested her cheek on his chest and smiled.

She didn't plan it, so she hadn't thought about it beforehand. But if this wasn't love, she couldn't imagine what was.

Tell your BFFs to meet you on Beacon Street!

Join the Tower Club at **BeaconStreetGirls.com** for Super-cool virtual sleepovers and parties!
Personalize your locker and get $5.00 to spend on Club BSG gifts
with this secret code

To get your $5 in MARTY☆MONEY (one per person) go to www.BeaconStreetGirls.com/redeem
and follow the instructions, while supplies last.